# BRIANA'S GIFT

# Lurlene McDaniel

# BRIANA'S GIFT

LAUREL-LEAF
BOOKS

Published by Laurel-Leaf
an imprint of Random House Children's Books
a division of Random House, Inc.
New York

Originally published in hardcover in the United States by Delacorte
Press, New York, in 2006. This edition published by arrangement
with Delacorte Press.

Laurel-Leaf and colophon are registered trademarks
of Random House, Inc.

www.randomhouse.com/teens
Educators and librarians, for a variety of teaching tools,
visit us at www.randomhouse.com/teachers

RL: 4.8
ISBN: 978-0-440-23869-0
March 2008
Printed in the United States of America
10 9 8 7 6 5 4 3 2 1
First Laurel-Leaf Edition

*This book is dedicated to the memory of
Noah Duble, age four, and to his family,
who will always love and miss him.*

*I wish to thank Dr. Lizabeth Kennedy, neonatologist at T. C. Thompson Children's Hospital in Chattanooga, for her excellent and invaluable input in helping me bring this story to life.*

*But Mary treasured up all these things and pondered them in her heart.*                    Luke 2:19 (NIV)

# ONE

I'm probably the only girl in the world who hates the month of December. I know Christmas comes in December, but so what? Every bad, awful thing that's ever happened in my family has happened in December. Like when I was five and Daddy died in an accident at the steel mill just two weeks before Christmas and we had to move to Tennessee and live with Grandma. And when I was eight and Mom was told in the first week of December she had rheumatoid arthritis and so she couldn't work and had to set up her own at-home business. And when I was almost fourteen, my sister, Briana, ran away from home on a cold December Saturday, just after school let out for the holiday break.

Mom said later, "I should have seen it coming."

But neither of us had.

Our mother always said that Briana marched to the beat of a different drummer, which I totally got because I'm in the marching band at school and staying in step is a must. When she was just sixteen, Bree took off with Jerry Stevens, a nineteen-year-old guy Mom called "worthless, hateful and without a lick of sense," but that Bree swore she loved more than anything. Bree and Mom had lots of fights about Bree dating Jerry, and then on a Saturday morning when Mom had driven into town to Pruitt's Food Mart for groceries, Bree comes down the stairs with two suitcases and a duffel bag and drops them at the front door.

"Where you going?" I ask. I'm sprawled on the sofa watching a cartoon and eating Cheetos. I like the old cartoons; plus, it's a good way to spend a Saturday until Mom makes me do my chores, which wasn't going to happen until she came home from the store. My fingers are covered with orange Cheetos dust and I lick them.

Bree scowls. "That's disgusting." She looks out the high glass window of the door. "I'm leaving."

"For where?"

"Los Angeles."

"Why?"

"Me and Jerry are going to find jobs."

"You don't know anyone in Los Angeles," I remind her. We live in farm country, in Duncanville, a small town in middle Tennessee, three hours from Nashville, only forty minutes from Chattanooga, which I guess Bree figures are both too close to home.

"We're going clear across country, seeing everything there is to see on the way. When we get to Hollywood, we'll get a place of our own and be happy forever." Her green eyes sparkle.

"Mom's not going to let you go." Bree had taken off twice before and Mom had gotten the sheriff to fetch her home.

"It's different this time."

"How so?"

"I left a letter in my room. It explains everything."

"What about school?"

"I'm finished with school. I can quit if I want to. You finish school."

"But——"

A horn honks outside and Bree throws open the door and grabs her bags. "I'm out of here."

I follow her onto the front porch, stop when I see Jerry's pickup in our dirt driveway. He jumps out, hugs Bree and tosses her bags into the open bed. "What did you pack, girl? The kitchen sink?" He never looks my way.

Bree laughs and kisses him. She says to me, "Go inside, Sissy."

I'm still wearing my sleep T-shirt and my legs and feet are bare. The cold has sliced right through me and frozen me to the porch.

Bree shoots Jerry an apologetic look, runs back and puts her arms around me. "It'll be all right, Sissy. I know what I'm doing."

I feel all hollow, scared too. I don't want my sister to leave.

"I'll send you postcards."

I stand still, my arms glued to my sides, fighting hard not to cry. I'm careful not to touch her with my disgusting orange fingers. "Why do you want to leave?"

"I don't want to be stuck in this place for-ever. This is my chance to go places with some-one I love and who loves me."

The truck's horn beeps and I see Jerry scowl-ing from behind the wheel. Bree breaks away. "I can't keep Jerry waiting." She bounds off the porch, runs to the truck, gets inside and rolls down the window. She calls out, "Tell Mom not to worry. I know what I want. I love you."

My voice is stuck in my throat and I can't say anything. I stand on the porch shivering and watch them drive away. And find another reason to hate December.

When Mom comes home, I tell her what's hap-pened and we go up to Bree's room together. The usually messy bedroom is neat and clean. The bed's made up with the old quilt Grandma sewed before she died and the closet holds only old summer T's and empty hangers. Mom picks up the letter propped on Bree's pillow. As I watch her stiffened fingers rip open the enve-lope, I cry. "Shush," she says, her eyes darting over the page.

"Wh-what's it say?"

"She and Jerry are getting married."

"Call the sheriff, Mom. You can stop them."

"Why? Once they're married, I have no say in her life."

"But school—"

"She's sixteen, Susanna. You can't stop a river from flowing downstream, and I can't stop Bree from going her own way. I should have seen it coming."

Shock waves roll over me. Briana is *gone.* Really and truly gone.

Mom gets to her feet and her orthopedic shoes shuffle on the wood floor. "Come on now and help me bring in the groceries."

*Bring in the groceries?* How can she think about groceries when her daughter, my only sister, has just run off to get married to a guy Mom hates? I swipe at my eyes. Mom puts her arm around my shoulder. "She'll be back, Sissy."

"When?"

"When he leaves her."

"But if they're married . . ."

"It's a lot easier to break promises than to keep them," Mom says. Her face looks sad. I still can't believe she isn't going to do anything to make Bree come back. "Come on now."

Mom shuts Bree's bedroom door behind us and we go downstairs.

I hardly remember living anyplace but Duncanville. We were in Indianapolis when Daddy fell to his death at the steel mill. Mom moved us to Grandma's farmhouse in the country in Duncanville where she'd grown up and told us it would be a nice place for us to grow up too. Not that we do any farming. When the doctors told Mom she had this bad kind of arthritis, she started a little bookkeeping business in the old sunroom at the back of the house. Grandma kept some chickens and a garden almost until the day she died, when I was ten. I missed Grandma a lot, and I think Bree did too, but she was too busy arguing and fighting with Mom about coming and going as she pleased to let us know it.

Bree hated our small school—all the grades are in the same building. I've never known any other kind, so I like Robert E. Lee Elementary, Middle and High School all in one, but Bree always said it was dull as dishwater and that kids in real cities were cool and not hicks. She bought teen magazines about cool kids in cool places and read them for hours.

I have two best friends, Melody Wallace and Stuart Ableman. We've been all through school together, same grade, same classroom even. In middle school, there are two eighth-grade classes, so Stuart got split off from us, but we still all do band together. We have a football team—JV and varsity rolled together, and we only play the little schools like us. Sometimes we have to travel on one old school bus—the players, the band, the coaches and the chaperones too.

Once word gets around that Bree Scanland has run off with Jerry, I'm asked a lot of questions, none of which I can answer. Nobody acts real shocked either. Guess it was well known around Duncanville that Bree marched to the beat of that different drummer.

She does send me postcards like she promised. At first anyway. They're postmarked Nashville, Oklahoma, Nevada and finally Los Angeles. They come often at first, then dribble down to a few, then none come at all. At first her postcards tell me about the fun she's having. Her last one just says, "L.A. is big and crowded." I stick it on my bulletin board with the others. I have a million questions for her. Does she have a job? Does she miss us? Does she like being married? I want her to call home, but she doesn't, not even on my birthday.

"She ever coming back?" Melody often asks. She has three brothers and they give her fits, and she says she wouldn't miss them if they left home.

"Maybe she'll get discovered in Hollywood," Stu says.

It's August, and Bree's been gone eight whole months. We're all fourteen—I turned fourteen in March, Melody in May and Stu in July. School's starting in another ten days, and we've just watched a TV movie at my house about girls getting murdered in L.A. "She's not dead, Stu. No one's *discovered* her body."

"I meant *discovered* her in a good way and made her into a movie star. It happens, you know. I read about it. She'd make a good movie star. And because she's your sister and we're your friends, we could all go out to Hollywood and see her. Maybe she'll introduce us around. Take us to her studio while she's making a picture."

He could make me crazy sometimes with his

imagination. "Bree won't become a movie star without telling me and Mom first thing."

"If she gets to be a star and wins an Academy Award, will she thank all us little people?" Melody was getting into Stu's stupid fantasy.

"Why should she? We didn't do anything to help her get to Hollywood," I say.

"Plus, Jerry might not let her talk to all of us ever again," Melody adds.

"Jerry's got no say. He was just a means to an end—getting her to Hollywood."

"You think she'll divorce him once she's rich and famous?" Stu asks. "That's not nice."

"Stars don't have to be nice. They just have to be stars." I stand up from where I've been sitting on the floor in front of the TV. "Look, I've got to start supper." Mom is working on a big project that came in this morning and it's my job to get supper going.

"Well, don't get all crabby," Melody says.

I don't like talking about my sister and making up stories about her. I miss her and only want to see her again. "I'm not crabby. I just need to start cooking."

"At four?"

"Mom likes to eat early."

I watch them leave, feeling deceitful, but also wanting to be by myself. At the end of our front yard, Stu turns. "See you in the morning?"

Like football practice, band practice has also started up. Mr. Mendoza insists that we march in the early morning before the day gets too hot. Stu's mom drives us to the football field and Melody's mom picks us up. "I'll be ready and waiting."

We've all gotten our driving permits, but we can't get our licenses until we're sixteen, so we get from place to place as best we can. Melody and Stu straddle their separate bikes for the half-mile ride into town, where they live. "You're not mad, are you? About Briana, I mean. We were just speculating and making up stories," Stu says. "Joking."

"I'm not mad."

I go inside and rattle around the kitchen. It really *is* too early to start supper, but I dig out pots and pans anyway. The house is quiet, and so when I hear a motor chugging up our long dirt driveway, I'm thinking it's UPS or FedEx for Mom. I walk out to the porch and see the cab of an unfamiliar semitruck rumbling in our yard, belching diesel smoke. I'm about to yell for Mom when the door on the passenger side swings open and Briana snakes down from the seat.

My mouth drops open and I just stare, not believing my eyes. Did we somehow conjure her up with our crazy Hollywood story?

# TWO

I fly off the porch and throw my arms around her just as the driver drops a battered suitcase at her feet. "Here you go, little lady," he tells Bree.

"Thanks for the ride."

Questions are bubbling out of my mouth, but Bree ignores them and watches the driver pull away. I take a good look at her. She looks tired and rumpled—bedraggled, Grandma would have said, like something the cat dragged in.

"You're home, Bree! We've really missed you. Tell me everything! Where's Jerry?" I say *we* because I know Mom has missed her even though we didn't talk about it. Sometimes I'd see her standing on the porch, or at a window staring down our country road, and I could just feel her wondering about Bree, where she was and if she was happy.

"Not now, Sissy. Is Mom around?"

Mom is standing on the front porch, staring hard at Bree and me.

Bree looks up at Mom, her eyes full of tears. I feel her muscles tense. She clears her throat. "Can I come home, Mom? Just for a little while?"

I figure it cost Bree a lot of pride to ask, but from the way she looks she isn't high on pride. I remember how she left—all full of smiles and with shining eyes.

Mom's mouth is set in a thin line, but I see tears in her eyes too. "Come on inside," she says. "Sissy, bring her bag."

I pick up the old suitcase, curious about my sister's homecoming and subdued by Mom's lack of enthusiasm. Still, my heart's happy. Bree's home!

Once on the porch, Mom and Bree regard each other like wary cats instead of blood kin. "When did you last eat?" Mom asks.

"This morning."

"You been traveling long?"

"Five days. I started from L.A. I had bus fare to Memphis. I hitched the rest of the way."

Mom looks dismayed. "Oh, Briana. That's so dangerous. Why didn't you call? I would have sent you money for the bus."

Bree's lips tremble and then she breaks down. Mom gathers her in her arms and rocks her while Bree sobs so hard her body shakes, and this makes me cry too.

"Come inside," Mom says. "Sissy, stop your crying and set another place for dinner."

I sniff hard. "Sure. I can make her bed up too." To Bree, I say, "Your room's just the way you left it."

Bree gives me a cautionary glance, chews on her bottom lip. "I-I don't want to put you-all to any trouble."

I think about all the arguing and yelling she and Mom went through just the summer before. This is a changed Bree and I hope Mom can see that. "You're my daughter, Bree. It's all right to come home," Mom says.

Tears have washed my sister's face clean, but

her eyes look sad, troubled. "I have to tell you something."

"Later," Mom says. "Go get a hot bath while we put supper on the table."

I'm disappointed. I don't want to wait. I want to hear everything Bree has to say right this minute.

Mom gives Bree's baggy clothes a long look. "You have any clean clothes in that suitcase?"

Bree shakes her head. I chime in with "She has some clean T-shirts in her closet and I have a pair of her jeans I can give back."

"That'll be fine," Mom says.

We go inside the house, watch Bree climb the stairs. She looks smaller somehow, with no bounce, like a balloon with its air let out. Mom turns to me and says, "Let's hurry supper, Sissy . . . get something ready to eat before the girl faints dead away."

Supper's quiet except for the clicking of our silverware. I want to talk, ask questions, but neither Bree nor Mom seems anxious to do so. Finally tired of hearing nothing but our forks, I ask, "Where's Jerry? He go home too?"

Mom shoots me a *hush up* signal, but I ignore it. I want to get Bree and Mom talking.

"Jerry and I broke up in L.A.," Bree says.

"Did you get a divorce?" Has my sister already gotten married and divorced before turning eighteen?

Bree puts down her fork, folds her hands in her lap. "We never got married."

"Oh," I say.

Mom says nothing.

Bree says, "Can I be excused?"

Another shock to my system—Bree's never asked permission for anything. She just does what she wants.

"You need to eat more. I'll keep your plate warm," Mom says. We watch Bree leave the kitchen. Mom says to me, "It's best to keep questions for your sister to yourself. Don't put her through the third degree. She'll talk when she wants to."

"Can I even say she's home? To my friends, I mean."

"I expect the whole town will know soon enough."

"But my friends—"

"Sissy, hush. You're giving me a headache. Just do what I tell you. Please."

Mom walks out of the kitchen too, leaving me to put away the food and clean up. I'm glad to keep busy. Something has gone really wrong in Bree's life. Something that a few days in her old room and some hot meals aren't going to fix.

"I heard Bree came home."

These are the first words from Melody's mouth once we get out of Stu's mother's car the next morning. We are trudging across the football field to where the marching band is gathering for its morning practice.

"Where'd you hear that?" Melody has looked ready to bust during the whole ride and now that I know what's on her mind, I'm irked. How did the news get around without me saying a single word?

"Mrs. Taylor saw her riding in a truck down Main Street, heading out toward your house," Melody says. "She called my mom last night and Mom asked me about it this morning."

"Hey, wait up!" Stu comes running behind us, juggling his trumpet case, which was locked in the car's trunk.

We stop and wait for him to catch up. Melody plays clarinet and I play flute. When he reaches us, Melody explains, "I was asking Sissy about Bree coming home."

"Bree's back?"

Just last night I was excited about telling them, but knowing Mrs. Taylor, Duncanville's biggest busybody, has already spread it around the whole town makes me protective of my sister's private business. "Yes," I say, then button my lips.

"Well, how is she? Did she say anything about Hollywood?"

"She was tired, Stu. She ate dinner and went to bed. We didn't talk much."

"You don't have to bite my head off."

"I just don't have anything to say yet. Can we just do band practice?"

"And Jerry?" Melody asks. "Where's he? Mom said that according to Mrs. Taylor, he wasn't with her in the truck."

"He wasn't?" Stu asks, drilling me with his blue eyes.

Just then Mr. Mendoza blows his whistle to signal us to line up in formation. "Let's get a move on, people," he yells. "Heat's rising."

I ignore Stu and step around Melody and fall into my marching space. Our director's right— the heat *is* building up. And not just the air temperature either. My heat's up because I don't like anyone, not even my friends, talking about my family. And I know that the inquisitive factor concerning Bree is going to be red-hot in Duncanville over the coming days. I can feel it already.

By the time practice is over, we're all dripping with sweat. Melody's mom picks us up and both Melody and Stu begin making plans to go to the city pool this afternoon. "I'll pack sandwiches," Melody says. "Stu, bring colas. You coming, Sissy?"

"Not sure."

"We'll meet in the park at noon," she instructs me. "If you're not there by twelve-thirty, we'll eat and go to the pool without you."

I know she's miffed because I haven't been forthcoming about Bree. I don't care. I honestly don't know much more, other than Bree and Jerry never getting married. Bad news that I want to keep to myself for a while.

Melody's mother lets me off and I walk up our long driveway kicking up dust. Bree's sitting on the porch snapping green beans and tossing them into Mom's old dented kitchen pot that she's holding between her knees.

"Hey," I say, coming up on the porch.

"Hey yourself." She looks a mess. No makeup and her hair a mass of wild frizz. The old Bree used to work for hours taming her hair, smoothing it so that it fell in waves. She hated the frizzies.

"Mom inside?"

"In her office."

I shift from foot to foot, feeling awkward and self-conscious in front of my own sister.

"You still play?" She glances at my flute case and asks the obvious.

"I'm head flutist. Ninth grade too." Maybe she's forgotten.

"I remember ninth grade. Bill Gorskey was crazy for me."

"You here to stay?" I blurt, in no mood for small talk.

"It depends."

"On what?"

She slumps backward in her chair. "You may as well sit down, Sissy. I've got some things to tell you."

My heart thumps and I sit on the floor cross-legged in front of her. "I'm listening."

"Do you think I want to be back here?"

"I—I don't know. Don't you?"

"Do you think I would have come if I'd had a choice?"

That hurts me. What's so horrible about living with me and Mom? "So why did you come home? Especially if you didn't want to?"

Moisture fills her eyes. "I'm pregnant, Sissy. I'm a cliché—barefoot and pregnant, with no place else to go."

# THREE

"Pregnant! But you're not married." As soon as the words are out of my mouth, I bite my tongue. What a stupid thing to say! I feel my face go flaming red. "Sorry," I say. "I must have had a brain disconnect. What does Jerry say about the baby?"

"He was all right about it at first. Then I started getting sick and I couldn't work. He—he left me in L.A. Said he wasn't ready to be a daddy and that he was tired of me too."

"That wasn't very nice."

"Turns out, Jerry wasn't very nice about much of anything." She snaps a bean with a vengeance.

23

"So . . . now what?"

"I don't know."

"What's Mom say?"

"She says we need to talk about my 'options.'"

I've had sex education in school so I know what her options are. I swallow hard. "You're not going to . . . I mean, you're not thinking about—"

"I—I don't know what I want to do. I'm tired of thinking about it!" Bree turns pale. "I'm going to be sick." She stands and the pot in her lap hits the porch floor with a thud. Beans scatter every which way, but Bree runs into the house and the screen door clatters behind her. With shaking hands, I crawl across the porch and gather up the glistening, fragile beans, fresh from their pods.

I arrive at the pool late, missing lunch with Stu and Melody, who are already swimming—splashing, actually. There must be fifty kids in the water. "We didn't think you were coming," Stu calls from the center of the melee.

"Chores," I say, knowing it isn't true, but

unwilling to shout out what's going on at my house, where Bree has retreated to her room and Mom is holed up in her office. It's taken me over twenty minutes to bike into town and I'm hot and sweaty.

"Come on in," Stu says.

I think I see the slightest hint of disappointment on Melody's face, but then she smiles. "I saved you half a sandwich."

"I'll eat it later." I hurry and change into my swimsuit in the locker room, shower to wash off the road dust and am heading out to the pool when Angie Simpson stops me.

"Can I ask you something?"

I freeze. I sure don't want to face questions about Bree. "What?"

"You're friends with Stuart Ableman, aren't you?"

"What about him?"

"Do him and Melody have a thing?"

"A *thing*?" The question catches me totally off guard.

"You know, are they together? Is he her BF?"

"We're all just friends. Why do you want to know?"

She giggles. "I think he's cute."

"Stu? Are you serious?"

"Don't you?"

I shrug.

She rolls her eyes at me. "Forget I asked."

"It's forgotten." I trudge outside into the heat, squinting because the light off the concrete is blinding. So Angie thinks Stu's cute. I look for my friends in the pool and find them on beach towels near the fence, both reading—Melody a romance novel and Stu a biography of some general from World War II. He has weird taste in books. I watch as Melody says something to him and Stu begins to rub suntan lotion on her back.

Stu has shot up during the summer and now he's taller than me or Melody. His hair's blonder since he's been in the sun so much, and I already know that his eyes are cornflower blue. I guess I can see why Angie said he was cute. I think about telling them what Angie said, then decide not to. Maybe Angie will make a move on him and Melody and I can tease him about it. We'll have a great laugh, tease him until he turns beet red.

I can hear Mom and Bree arguing all the way up in my bedroom. I open the door slightly and stand with my ear to the crack. "You need a plan, Bree," Mom is saying.

"Well, I don't have one." Bree sounds snarly.

"If you're keeping the baby, make Jerry pay child support."

"I don't want Jerry anywhere near me and my baby."

"It's not just your baby, Briana. It's his too. He's responsible."

"Like he cares."

"So what *are* your plans?"

"I told you, I don't have any yet."

"Where do you plan to live?"

Silence. Bree finally says, "You want me to leave?"

My heart hammers.

"No," Mom says. She sounds tired. "But Bree, I can't take care of a newborn."

"Have I asked you to?"

"You need a job."

"I'll get a job."

"But if you're working full-time, who will take care of the baby? This isn't a doll you can pick up and put down anytime you feel like it. It's a baby! It will have colic, cry at night, keep you awake. You'll have to buy diapers, bottles, a crib—babies *need* stuff, and stuff costs money. How will you pay for everything? I'm still caring for your sister."

I hear Bree slam something on the kitchen table. "Will you stop with all these questions! I—I can't think. Just get off my back!"

I hear a door slam and know that Bree has left the house—not that she has anywhere to go without a car. I close my bedroom door and get out my flute. Music always takes my mind out of the moment and into a private place. I play until I feel calm, until I feel like the world isn't spinning out of control.

On the Friday morning before school starts, Mom rousts me out of bed before eight in the morning. "Get dressed," she says. "We're going into Chattanooga."

"Why can't I stay here?" I pull the pillow over my head.

Mom yanks it off, and in a voice that gives no room for protesting says, "Bree's got an appointment with an obstetrician at the health department and you're coming with us."

No one says anything at all during the forty-minute ride through the rolling hills into the city. Bree stares out the window and Mom keeps her gaze glued to the road. I sit in the backseat picking off my nail polish.

The health department is in a small building right next to the city's biggest hospital. We park and go inside, sign in, are handed a fistful of paperwork to fill out, and find seats in a waiting area crowded with people, kids and crying babies. Bree sits stony-faced and I rifle through an ancient, dog-eared *Time* magazine. By the time Bree gets called, it's almost noon.

Mom insists we all go to the exam room, where we meet a woman obstetrician named Dr. Wehrenberg. She gives me a questioning look and Mom says, "I want Sissy to hear what you have to say."

I get hot all over because she's practically announced that she doesn't want me to turn out the same way as Bree. *As if.* I've never even kissed a guy and can't think of a single boy I even want for a boyfriend. *Geez!* I stand to one side.

The exam room is small and brightly lit. There's a padded table with gizmos that look like upside-down stirrups. The doctor asks Bree, "Do you know how far along you are?"

"I wasn't keeping track of . . . things."

"We'll figure it out." The doctor makes notes in a manila folder.

"How old are you?"

"Seventeen."

The doctor scribbles some more, then says to Mom, "I need to do an exam. Afterward, we'll go into my office and talk. You and your other daughter can wait there for me. A nurse will show you the way."

Her office is piled with books and paper. Medical posters hang on the walls along with framed diplomas and certificates, all with names of different doctors. "She probably shares her office," I suggest, but Mom is in no mood for talking, so I sit on a chair and study a poster of a pregnant woman with a cutaway side view showing a full term, upside-down baby. I've read the labels for all of the woman's and the baby's body parts when Dr. Wehrenberg and Bree join us.

"Based on what Bree tells me," Dr. Wehrenberg says, pulling out the chair behind the desk, "she looks to be about sixteen or seventeen weeks along. Full term is forty weeks, so I'm estimating that the baby is due around mid-January. She's had no prenatal care thus far, so she needs to start immediately."

The doctor picks up a pad of paper and writes while she talks. "Prenatal vitamins to begin at once. A sonogram next week. Check-ups here once a month until she's seven months, then once a week until she delivers. Any hint of cramping or spotting, call me. I recommend attending labor and delivery classes—usually about six weeks before the birth. Will you be in the labor room with her?" The doctor looks at Mom.

"Seems so," Mom says, her lips tight around the words.

I feel like excess baggage.

The doctor looks directly at Bree. "It's important that you take care of yourself, Briana. The baby's growing and you need to be strong and healthy for a normal delivery. I'm giving you some brochures and a booklet that will help you understand what's happening to your body and how a baby develops."

Bree looks somber and says nothing.

I stop listening. Apparently my sister and mother have ruled out one "option." She is *going* to have the baby. This secretly pleases me. I, Susanna Margaret Scanland, am going to be an aunt. I can feed the baby a bottle, show it off to my friends, maybe even take it downtown in a stroller when it gets older. *Aunt Sissy.* I like the sound of it.

My ears prick up when the doctor says something about a sonogram. ". . . in a good position, we may be able to determine your baby's sex. Won't that be exciting?"

Bree looks dazed. Too much information, I figure.

Mom stands up. She looks grim, but also determined. "I'll have her here for every appointment."

We set up an appointment, leave the health department and drive back home, once more in total silence.

# FOUR

School starts on Monday. The halls are filled with the usual faces, but because we're in ninth grade—technically high school—we feel totally cooler than the middle-grade bottom-feeders. This year, it's Melody who is separated from me and Stu in homeroom, but we have two classes together, ending the day in band.

With the first football game looming, Mr. Mendoza steps up practices, which means that I don't get home until almost five, so Mom makes Bree responsible for starting supper, which she does without a fuss. She also lands a job as a cashier at the Super Wal-Mart out on Highway 111. I help Mom with the grocery shopping on Saturday. I push the basket while Mom rides around in one of those special motorized carts the store keeps on hand. Together we wait in Bree's line and let her check us out. She tries to act professional while ringing us up, but I make faces and talk in funny voices until I make her laugh.

On Labor Day weekend tons of stuff goes on sale. We buy some jeans and T's for me, a pair of Mary Janes, and for my bedroom, two Christmas cactuses that the saleslady in the garden department *swore* would bloom in December— something I can look forward to. Mom also buys some maternity clothes for Bree, who is popping out of her regular clothes. Her belly looks like a fat water balloon while the rest of her is skinny as ever.

When Bree brings home her first sonogram and shows it to me, I turn it round and round, but I can't see a baby in the dark blobs and smudges. "You sure this is a baby?"

She points to one dark spot in particular. "This is the head."

"If you say so."

She points again. "This is the spine."

"Is it a boy or girl?"

"The baby was turned wrong, so we can't tell yet. Maybe the next one will show its privates." She sticks the paper image on the refrigerator with a magnet.

Bree's getting into having the baby, something Mom still isn't happy about because Bree keeps refusing to make Jerry take responsibility. No one asks my opinion, but I think Bree is right. The guy is long gone out on the West Coast, and tracking him down seems more trouble than it's worth. His folks have moved away from Duncanville too, so it isn't as if finding him would be easy. I feel like we'll be fine— the baby, Bree, Mom and me, living in our house all together. The pictures in my head always show us smiling and playing with the baby. A far cry from the tension in the air around our home.

Our school's football team surprises us and makes it into the area play-offs in late September. The whole town catches the fever of winning and you can't go anywhere without hearing someone saying, "How about those Red Raiders!" What it means for our marching band is more formation practice and long trips to additional games. On the night of the big game between Duncanville and Shelbyville, Melody has the flu, so Stu and I end up riding the bus together without her. It feels awkward because Melody is sort of like the gas that drives our threesome. Not that I don't like being alone with Stu—I do—but he's changed over the summer. Not in a bad way; it's just that he's different, more sure of himself, more aware of what's going on around him. On the trip to the Shelbyville field, the whole bus is buzzing and I can cut the excitement with a knife.

"I saw Bree at the Wal-Mart on Saturday," Stu tells me. The bus is dark and his voice seems to float over me. "I'm thinking of filling out an application myself to work over the Christmas holidays." Stu is Jewish, so Christmas isn't a big event in his life.

"Because you want to buy me and Melody presents?"

He laughs. "I want to make more money than I do cutting grass. I thought if I worked over the holidays, it would be easier to land a job at the store next summer."

*That Stu. Always thinking.* "Sounds like a plan."
I realize that if he works next summer we won't
be hanging with each other as much. "I'd like to
get a summer job too," I say recklessly. In truth,
I haven't thought about it at all. "I want to
have money for clothes and to buy Bree's baby
pretty things. It's an aunt's responsibility, don't
you think?"

He shrugs. "I'm saving for college. Georgia
Tech. They have a great engineering school.
Where do you want to go to college?"

We've never talked about this kind of stuff
before. "Not sure yet," I say. I want him to think
I've actually given college a thought, which I
haven't.

"Melody says she's thinking about going to
the University of Georgia," he tells me.

*When did they talk about that?* I thought our
threesome talked about everything together. "So
I hear," I say, knowing I've never heard it from
her lips.

We're at Shelbyville High and the bus starts
unloading. The team trots off to the locker room
and our band trudges toward our designated
area in the bleachers, already filling up with

fans. Lights shine, making the grassy field bright
as day. The air is crisp and smells of burnt leaves.
I can see my breath as I huff up the steps. Across
the field, the Shelbyville cheerleaders are jumping up and down, and their band is giving an
impromptu rendition of a popular country song.

"They sound terrible," I say.

"They sound like us," Stu says, making me
laugh.

We are partway up when my foot slips on a
step and I tumble backward. Stu catches me and
saves me from falling. His strong arms right me
and I turn to thank him. Maybe it was a play of
the lights or the cool autumn night, I can't say,
but suddenly, I see him through new eyes. I look
up into the face of a blond, good-looking guy
with a square jaw and bright blue eyes. He's
both familiar and unfamiliar at the same time:
his face the same one from childhood, yet somehow different. His hair curls on his forehead. I
want to reach up and touch it. A funny flutter-
ing sensation sweeps through my stomach, and
my skin feels on fire.

"You okay?" Stu asks, looking concerned.

My breath stalls. "I—I'm fine," I stammer,

feeling dumber than a brick. *This is stupid!* This is *Stu*. We've been best friends forever.

He brushes my hair off my shoulder and rights my band sash.

My stomach does a flip-flop.

"You two want to move it!" Gilbert, our tuba player, shouts from behind us.

Quickly I turn and sprint up the steps and take my seat, my heart beating like a drum— not from exercise, but from some mysterious malady that struck me when I stared up into Stu's face. I fumble with my flute, wondering if I can catch my breath enough to blow into it. *I'm going crazy!* I think. All during the game, I wonder if these feelings would have happened if Melody had been on the bus with us. I have no way of knowing. And worse, I know there is no way I can tell her either. No way at all.

Our football team goes down in flames, even as I am going up in flames over Stuart Ableman— figuratively speaking. I come back down to earth during the week, after giving myself a couple of stern lectures and a reality check. We're friends. He's a boy, and my hormones, those pesky controllers of mood and body, are going full tilt inside me. I tell myself that I'm all caught up in Bree's situation and feeling gooey because babies make girls feel gooey.

On the very next sonogram Bree brings home, she points to a particular spot on the still indecipherable strip of paper and tells me and Mom, "It's a girl."

I could swear Mom's eyes mist over, but she shakes her head and asks, "How are you ever going to take care of her, Briana?"

"Thanks for the vote of confidence. Haven't I got a job? Aren't I doing all I can to help around here?"

She's right about that much. The old Bree, the one who liked to sneak out and run around with boys and who dropped out of school and never paid any attention to Mom's lectures, didn't come home that day in the truck. I think my sister is trying real hard to be a grown-up. She's stopped smoking too, but she's told me that she wants a cigarette bad and is planning on having one just as soon as the baby's born. It makes me glad I don't smoke because I wouldn't like something having a hold on me that way.

Mom says, "Yes, you're helping, but how long will that last? Babies are full-time, you know."

"Mom, please back off! I'm trying hard! Besides, what guy's going to look at me now? I waddle like a duck and I'm getting as big as a blimp."

"Maybe we should talk about fixing up a room for the baby," I interrupt, and they both look at me. I forge ahead. "Now that we know it's a girl, we can paint Grandma's old bedroom and turn it into a nursery. The baby should have a nice place to sleep in and play in, don't you think?"

Mom sighs and Bree folds her arms across her chest. "I already put a crib and baby furniture on hold at the Wal-Mart. I'm paying for everything myself." She adds the last part as a special dig at Mom.

"I'll paint the walls," I say eagerly. "We can pick out the color together." I painted my bedroom last spring, and the bright lime green color looks pretty enough to lick.

"I'm thinking about lavender," Bree says, turning toward me. "And maybe putting some of that lime green of yours on one wall. You have any left over?"

This is the first time Bree has made me feel like my ideas matter. She likes my color choices. "I have enough for one wall."

"Good. When I get off tomorrow, we'll choose the prettiest shade of lavender in the store."

Mom says, "The room has junk in it. It'll have to be cleared out before you paint."

I know that her underlying message is that she can't do it because of her arthritis, and that Bree shouldn't because of her pregnancy. "Stu and Melody and I'll do it." I volunteer my friends without hesitation, knowing they will help. And now that I've had a mental course correction in the way I think about Stu, it will be easier to be around him.

Mom nods. "Drag it all out to the barn. We'll have a yard sale in the spring." She leaves the room, limping from her bad knees.

On Saturday my friends show up, along with Melody's oldest brother, who's as big as a moose. We make short work of emptying out the room and finding space for the old furniture out in the barn. Mom feeds us cookies fresh from the oven; Bree stays out of the way. Whenever I'm near

Stu, my palms sweat and my heart beats faster. I figure I'm not as on top of my feelings as I thought. I'm careful not to look at him much—what if someone sees my silly crush stamped on my face?

I try talking my friends into staying on to help me paint, but neither Stu nor Melody will. "Other plans," they tell me.

Later I start taping the baseboards while Mom drives Bree to her job. I'm stirring a paint can containing a luscious shade of lavender when the doorbell rings. I gallop downstairs. Through the glass door, I see a woman with a briefcase in a business suit standing on the porch. She smiles at me through the glass, calls out, "Hello. I'm looking for Brenda Scanland."

"Mom will be right back," I tell her, remembering I'm never to let a stranger inside.

"Are you Briana?"

"She's my sister. Who are you?"

"Sheila Watson." She reaches into her briefcase, takes out a business card and presses it against the glass for me to see. It reads: SHEILA WATSON, ATTORNEY-AT-LAW.

# ❺❶❷❸

"Why would you *do* that?" Bree is shouting at Mom while I listen from my perch at the top of the stairs. "Why would you think I'd give up my baby?"

"It's only an option, Bree . . . something to consider. I'm not advocating private adoption, but maybe it's something you should explore."

"I won't! I'm keeping my baby and that's that."

I hear tears in Bree's voice, and my own heart is pounding. So that's what Sheila Watson and Mom discussed behind the closed door of Mom's office that afternoon! I couldn't hear a thing through the wood door—not that I didn't try—but they spoke quietly. Sometimes Mom's bookkeeping clients come to the house, but I knew deep down that Sheila Watson, Attorney-at-Law, was not one of Mom's clients. Now that I know why she came, I'm as shocked and angry as my sister.

"There are so many couples who can't have babies, Bree," Mom says, her voice calm and reasoning. "There are women who'd give anything to have a newborn of their own. They may have been on adoption agency waiting lists for years."

"You want me to *sell* my baby?" Bree screeches. "I'm not selling my baby to some lawyer!"

"Oh, stop it! Don't be dramatic. That's not what this is all about. The attorney is just a go-between for a birth mother and clients who desperately want a baby. They'll pay all your expenses and provide the baby with a good home. Ms. Watson explained that it can be an open adoption where you still have contact with your baby for as long as you like. You can even have some say in who gets your child. Ms. Watson says it's done all the time."

"Well, *not* by me! This is my baby, and I'm keeping her."

I hear Bree scrape back her kitchen chair, so I jump up and run into my room. I'm not proud of eavesdropping, but how else am I going to find out what's going on? I pace the floor, both scared and creeped out. What is Mom thinking to try and make Bree give up her baby to strangers? I'm going to be her aunt, but Mom is going to be her grandmother—Mom's first grandchild! We can't give her away like a kitten from an unwanted litter.

I hear Bree storm down the hall and slam into her bedroom. I pace, steaming about the conversation I've overheard. In desperation, I pick up my flute and play random pieces of music, put it down when I realize I'm playing one of my earliest practice pieces—"Three Blind Mice." Is that what we are? Three people who can't see things the way they are? Is Mom right? Can Bree really raise a baby? Will she get tired of the responsibility? And how about Bree's feelings? Can she truly take care of a child for eighteen years? That's a long time for her to be "responsible." And why are they ignoring me?

Don't they know how much I want to be a part of the baby's life?

I put down my flute, glance at my Christmas cactuses sitting in pots on my windowsill. With a jolt, I see that they look droopy, and I quickly poke a finger into the soil. Dry as a bone. I rush the pots into the bathroom, hold them under the tap until each is soaked with water. "Perk up!" I command. "Don't you dare die on my watch."

With football season officially over, Mr. Mendoza trots out the music we'll be playing at the school's annual Christmas-Chanukah-Kwanza event. Duncanville's holiday extravaganza is the highlight of December in our little town and is performed on the Friday night preceding our long holiday break. The band, the chorus and all the classes from kindergarten through high school perform music, dances and skits in the city auditorium downtown, packed to overflowing by relatives and friends of the students. When the music is passed out in October, the entire band groans in unison.

"Isn't it too early for this stuff?" someone in the string section asks.

"I *hate* this music," another person grumbles.

I'm already dreading hearing and playing "Santa Claus Is Coming to Town" umpteen times.

"Can't we do some Christmas carols?" Trudy McClellan asks. She's very religious.

"You know we can't," Mr. Mendoza says. "But cheer up. This year we're going to do a few pieces from *The Nutcracker*."

This makes all of us feel better. Tchaikovsky is a whole lot more challenging than "Rudolph the Red-Nosed Reindeer." And *The Nutcracker* has some great parts for flute and piccolo, an instrument I also play. We work on the music every day during class, and I practice it at home too. By two weeks before Halloween, I can play my part from the Chinese dance segment perfectly. Oh, and my Christmas cactuses have revived too. By the end of October, I also have my feelings for Stu back under control. In short, I'm feeling pretty good inside and out.

"You want me to get us some DVDs so we can watch movies tomorrow night?" Melody and I are waiting by the gym for her mom to pick us up after school. Halloween is this weekend, but we're too old for trick-or-treating. We did the scary movie thing last year with Stu and really had a good time.

"I heard Mom and Dad making some family plans," Melody says vaguely.

"Maybe Stu would like to watch movies with me."

"He told me his parents were having friends over for a dinner party."

This is news. I haven't figured on *not* being with my friends on Halloween night. "You mean I'm stuck at my house? You know no one comes to our place." We live far enough out of town that kids never come our way. Over the years it's saved Mom a fortune in candy costs, but left me to either be with Mom and Bree or go into town to hang with my friends. And now that option is closing. "You're dooming me to aloneness!"

"Sorry," Melody says. "I can't help it."

"This stinks!"

"Come over Sunday afternoon. I'll be home all day."

"What fun is that? Watching scary movies in broad daylight."

Melody shrugs, looks genuinely sorry. "I'll call you if my plans change."

"Why can't you and Stu come to my house?" I get the feeling Melody isn't telling me everything.

"I told you, I have to be with my family. And Stu said his folks expect him to pass out candy during the dinner party." It makes sense, but I still don't like it. I'm working on a good sulk when Melody asks, "How's Bree doing? When's her baby due? You said it was a girl. Has she picked a name?"

Melody's just trying to make up with me—I recognize the tactic of asking a ton of enthusiastic questions to make another person feel better after being shot down. "She hasn't decided on a name yet, but she's got until January," I say coolly.

Just a week ago, Bree had read a part from her "how babies develop" book aloud to me, which said that at twenty-four weeks a baby's "auditory functions are completely formed. They can hear your voice and respond to music, which calms them."

"That's cool," I told my sister.

"All she's hearing is the sound of the Wal-Mart cash register opening and closing," Bree noted.

"What else?" I asked.

"'At twenty-nine weeks, your baby can remember the music you play during your pregnancy after she's born.'" Bree read. "Gee, who knew? Maybe I should pick out some new tunes and listen to them. You know, some classical stuff. You got some CDs?"

Struck by a sudden inspiration, I said, "I'll play my flute for her."

"Try it. She's jumping all over the place and I need some sleep. It's hard to sleep when something's trying to kick its way out of you."

I got my flute and, holding it close to Bree's tummy, I played a couple of soothing songs. "It's working," Bree said, looking surprised and cupping her hands under her swollen belly. I played more music until Bree insisted that the baby had stopped hopping around. "Thanks, Sissy." Knowing I'd helped pleased me. So now I play for the baby whenever she's especially restless, or if Bree asks me to.

I decide against telling Melody any of this. Why should I? My friends are deserting me on Halloween and all Melody can say is "sorry." Plus, I'm working to keep my feelings about Stu in check, mostly because I don't want Melody teasing me about it. Stu isn't exactly Mr. Warmth around me these days either. I can't put my finger on what's going on with the three of us, but something is different. Sure, we still do things together, but something has changed since the summer. I sense it like a deer senses danger. I just can't figure out what it is.

So I stay home on Halloween feeling sorry for myself. Bree is working an extra shift at Wal-Mart, and Mom's watching some old crybaby movie on TV. She asks me, "Do I need to run you over to Melody's?"

How bad is it when your mother notices that you're excess baggage? "Not necessary," I tell her. "She's doing something else. Family stuff."

"Oh." Mom turns back to the TV. "You want to watch this movie with me? It's a classic."

"Naw. I think I'm going to paint the wood-work in the baby's room."

"I thought you decided against doing that. Too much work."

"I changed my mind." I really hate the tedious job of painting baseboards on my hands and knees, but I'm really bored. So I go upstairs, drag out my painting supplies and am putting on a fresh coat of white paint when I hear the phone ring downstairs. For a brief second, I imagine it's Melody or Stu offering me a reprieve, but seconds later I hear Mom yell, "Sissy, come quick! Bree collapsed at the Wal-Mart and an ambulance is taking her to the hospital in Chattanooga!"

# SIX

"What happened to her?" We're in the car, hurtling through the night toward Chattanooga.

"I don't know. All her manager said was that she collapsed at the cash register. The paramedics were called and they worked on her, then put her into an ambulance and headed for the city."

In the headlights of the few cars that pass us on the highway through the mountains, I see Mom's frantic expression. I ask, "Do you think it has anything to do with her baby?"

"I don't know, Sissy! Stop asking me questions I can't answer."

Tears slide silently down my cheeks. How can this be happening? What's wrong with my sister? Will her baby be all right? I bite my tongue to keep from asking anything else.

I've never seen Mom drive so fast, and the usual forty-minute ride only takes us twenty-eight. We squeal into the hospital's ER parking lot, hurry into the waiting area, me running, Mom limping behind. She tells the admittance nurse who she is and asks Briana's whereabouts. The nurse lifts a phone receiver and makes a call. "Have a seat," she says. "Someone will be down in a minute."

"Down from where? I thought she was in the ER."

"She's been taken upstairs, Mrs. Scanland, into ICU."

"She was pregnant. Do you know—"

"I don't know anything," the nurse says sympathetically. "Please just wait for the doctor."

We stand like statues, and people in the waiting area stare at us. A little boy is dressed up like a goblin, clutching a jack-o'-lantern candy pail and wearing a makeshift sling on one arm. A man wearing a Zorro costume holds crutches between his legs. Just an hour ago I was feeling sorry for myself because I was stuck at home. Now I'm glad I was at the house, not over at Melody's watching movies and believing that our world was in order when it wasn't.

A man arrives, introduces himself as Dr. Franklin and takes us to a staff elevator. The ride is freaky because no one says a word, and when we step into a dimly lit hallway, we face a door sign reading: NEUROLOGY ICU. Dr. Franklin says, "Before I take you in to see your daughter, we need to talk." He leads us into a small cubicle, sits us down.

"It's bad, isn't it?" Mom asks.

"We're still running tests, but yes."

He doesn't even bother to say soothing words. I hold my breath.

Dr. Franklin leans forward, his hands pressed together like someone in prayer. "There's no way to sugarcoat this. A blood vessel has burst in your daughter's brain—an aneurysm. Apparently it was a congenital defect, totally undetectable until now. Sort of a mini time bomb she's carried since birth."

I struggle to grasp his explanation. *A bomb went off inside Bree's head?*

"It can happen to anyone. One day, often without warning, the vessel pops and the person—" He stops the explanation and in the silence even I understand what he's telling us.

"Briana's *dead?*" Mom's voice quivers. "My daughter is *dead?*"

"An MRI shows massive irreversible bleeding in her brain. And her eyes are fixed and dilated. Her pupils don't react when I shine a light in them."

"Can't you fix her?" I don't realize I've spoken until they both look at me.

Dr. Franklin shakes his head. "We can't."

"And her baby?" Mom asks.

"That's what I want to talk to you about." He waves his hand, and almost at once, a woman enters the cubicle, closing us in like a spider snagging flies.

She manages a smile, holds out her hand, introduces herself as Dr. Kendrow, head of neonatal intensive care for the hospital. I can't get my mind around what Dr. Franklin has said, and now there's another doctor to face. "The baby's alive and well," Dr. Kendrow says. "Briana's on a ventilator and that's keeping her organs working. Her heart's strong and young. Youth is on her side. As long as she's kept alive, as long as she remains on the vent, the baby will be safe."

Mom looks frightened, and as pale as paper. "Okay."

I'm still digesting the news that the baby's all right, and that a machine is keeping my sister's body working normally. It sounds like something in a sci-fi movie.

Dr. Kendrow reaches for Mom's hand, holds it loosely in hers. "We estimate the baby to be around twenty-eight to twenty-nine weeks old— too young, too underdeveloped to be born healthy right now. If we perform a C-section tonight, the baby has a poor chance of surviving. Or if she survives, she'll spend months in ICU and could be permanently handicapped."

Fresh tears sting my eyes. My sister is dead and her baby is doomed.

"And if you don't do the C-section?" Mom's voice is trembling.

"I'm suggesting that Briana remain on the vent for as long as possible. To give her baby a chance to continue developing. Because every day, every hour, every minute the baby can remain *in utero,* the better her chances for living a normal life once she's born."

I think about what she's saying. A life without a mother. How normal is that? Then I recall the times Mom has encouraged Bree to give up her baby. I hear their arguments. I see the lawyer who came to our home, remember all the times Mom wanted Bree to track down Jerry. My heart pounds and my palms are soaked with sweat. It's Mom's decision! Bree's baby's life lies in my mother's arthritis-crippled hands.

She says nothing and I stare at her, waiting for some cue, some kind of signal that she won't do the unthinkable.

Dr. Kendrow says, "This isn't without precedent, Mrs. Scanland. In other cases, medical science has kept pregnant women in comas hydrated and nourished until their babies were ready for delivery. We can do the same for your daughter."

"And then?" Mom's voice falls to a whisper.

"And then we turn off the machines," Dr. Franklin says, "and allow her body to join her spirit."

The air in the cubicle has grown stale and for a moment I feel dizzy.

Mom struggles to her feet. "I want to see my daughter."

I jump up beside her. "Me too."

Dr. Franklin nods. "Of course. But let me emphasize . . . no matter how good she looks to you, a machine is doing the work of Briana's lungs and is keeping her alive. "

The inside of the unit looks like the images I've seen on TV of a space station. A desk in the center is lined with monitors and machines, peopled by nurses dressed in green lookalike clothing. Beds seem to float in the semidarkness, the patients tethered by wires, cords and IV lines. The room sounds mechanical, a spaceship housing human life-forms caught in some weird medical dance. Briana's bed is pushed off to one side near a wall beside a machine that hisses rhythmically. She lies flat, a contraption taped over her mouth with a hose linking her to the raspy machine.

She looks exactly like she's sleeping, a princess waiting for her Prince Charming to come and wake her with a kiss. Her hair sprays out wildly on the pillow, her eyes are closed, her belly a swollen mound beneath the covers. Her skin is pale; her hands lie flat on the bed on either side of her body, the nails glowing vivid pink with Luscious Flamingo, her newest favorite shade of polish. I watched her paint it on two nights ago. She's still wearing her Wal-Mart uniform.

I fight to get my head around the idea that although she looks alive, she isn't. How can the doctor be so sure? Tests can be wrong! Last year Melody's mother was told that she had breast cancer. But she didn't. The lumps were cysts. I remember crying with my friend, then jumping up and down for joy when the truth came out.

I watch Mom pick up Bree's hand and squeeze it. Bree's fingers are limp and unresponsive. Mom chokes out, "Oh, my poor baby girl."

I've seen Mom cry over Bree, her wild child, but this time it's different. Long ago, Mom was pregnant with both Bree and me. Inside Bree's body, another baby girl lies waiting to be born. That truth twists in me like a knife. I want to save her, keep her safe.

Dr. Kendrow says, "If you decide to maintain

your daughter for the sake of the baby, we'll do a tracheotomy and place the vent tube into her throat. That way her face won't be obscured by any medical devices."

Is this the doctor's way of saying that Bree will look like herself? I think about her being nothing more than a mechanical windup doll, everything looking normal, but without the spark of life. It seems impossible. My tears plop on top of the covers, making a water stain on the dry fabric. I don't even bother to wipe my eyes. I don't care if the moisture soaks clear through to Bree's skin. She'll never feel it.

Mom says, "She has an obstetrician. . . ."

"We'll handle everything," Dr. Kendrow says. "You're Bree's mother and she's a minor. You can speak for her."

Mom's hand begins moving tenderly over the contours of Bree's body. I'm staring at my sister's abdomen. The blanket jiggles, startling both of us. My breath catches in my throat and I want to shout, *See! You're wrong! She's not dead!*

"The baby's moving," Dr. Kendrow says.

My heart sinks as I recall watching Bree's belly jump while she watched TV beside me on the sofa, and how she would groan and say, "She's on the move. I'll never get to sleep tonight."

I place my open hand atop the blanket spread across Bree's belly, feel the quivering movement shiver against my palm. Mom puts her hand on mine. Our eyes lock. My mother says, "Keep the baby inside her. Give her every chance to live."

I'm so grateful that I cry fresh tears.

# SEVEN

News about Bree spreads like lightning and within twenty-four hours, casseroles, fresh-baked bread, homemade cookies, cakes and pies begin to appear on our porch. People we hardly know send us cards, notes and flowers. Employees from Wal-Mart show up with a truck on Saturday and unload every piece of nursery furniture that Bree had put on hold at the store.

"We all chipped in and paid for it," her manager explains to us. "We'd like to set it up for her baby in the nursery. Bree told us all how pretty it is. We're real sorry about what's happened to her. Maybe someday her baby will know that her mother chose this just for her. You'll tell her, won't you?" Mom and I say we will.

At school, Melody and Stu surround me. They chase away nosy kids with dumb questions, answer questions from teachers and the front office so I don't have to and help organize a special table in front of the school office for a Bree fund.

My problem is that I start crying when I least expect it. I leave the music room twice when we're rehearsing the Christmas music. The second time, Mr. Mendoza follows me out. "Susanna, do you want out of the Christmas program? It's all right if you do. Tiffany Banks can take over your instruments' parts."

*Tiffany Banks!* She can't play a radio! "I—I can do it, Mr. Mendoza," I say. "It gives me something to look forward to, you know?" It's a white lie, but learning the complicated pieces from *The Nutcracker* keeps my mind busy with something other than my sister and her baby.

He nods. "Listen, Susanna, I'm really sorry about your sister."

Instantly tears spring to my eyes.

He looks at the floor. "Okay. Back to work." I know he doesn't know what else to say. Who does? What *can* anyone say when a seventeen-year-old girl is declared brain-dead in the prime of her life?

Melody comes over one afternoon, and when Mom goes out, we creep into Briana's bedroom. I haven't been inside since her incident, which is what they call it at the hospital. Mom has shut the door and has told me, "We'll deal with this later." My sister's room is a wreck. We see clothes tossed everywhere, the bed unmade, a few kitchen plates with dried food (and ants) and her CD collection stacked atop her dresser on her bedside table and on the floor. "Whoa," Melody says. "Major earthquake."

To me it looks as if Briana will be back any minute. When she ran off with Jerry, the room looked sterile and picked over, everything neat and tidy. This scene is the real Briana, and that makes my heart hurt. I begin picking up her clothes, which I either hang up or put away in her dresser.

"Should I help?" Melody asks. She stands in the doorway, looking nervous.

"I'll do it." There's something I want from the room, and picking up stuff will help me find it.

"Are you sure we should be in here?"

"Why not? It's my sister's room."

"Yes, but—"

"If you don't want to be in here with me, wait in my room," I say, cutting her off.

"No. I—it's just kind of freaky, that's all."

"Not for me. It's just stuff, Mellie. It's not like she's lying in the bed watching us."

We both stare at the bed, half expecting Briana to rear up from under the covers.

"If you say so." Melody wanders around as if she were lost, while I keep working. "What will you do with her stuff?"

"No idea."

"You all can probably sell a lot of it on eBay."

I give her a wilting look. "We're not selling Bree's things on eBay."

Melody blushes. "I guess I shouldn't have said that."

"No. You shouldn't have." I throw off Bree's bedcovers and find what I've been searching for buried under her pillow.

"What's that?"

"Bree's booklet about pregnancy called *Watch*

*Me Grow.* It tells what's going on with a baby inside the mother week by week."

"Let me see." She leans over my shoulder.

This irritates me, but I flip through the booklet and stop at a line drawing of an upside-down baby curled into a ball, its arms crossed and its legs folded against its chest.

"What's it say?"

"It says, 'By week thirty-one your baby's turned around and head down, getting ready to be born.' It says that 'the fetus secretes a liquid from a new cell layer that prepares it to breathe air when it's born.'"

"So it's breathing water now? Like a fish?"

I roll my eyes. Melody knows so little about babies *in utero.* "Babies aren't fish. They can't breathe at all until they're born."

"But it's still too soon for her to be born, isn't it?"

I nod. "She doesn't weigh very much and her lungs need more time to develop. Bree and I keep—" I stop myself. "We kept track of how her baby was growing together. Did you know that a baby can hear noises when it's inside its mother?"

Melody shakes her head. "That's awesome. What else?"

I notice that Bree has made notes in the margins of the book—things like *I'm getting so fat* and *It's a girl and she'll wear pink and green every day. Hope she gets Sissy's hair, not kinky like her mama's,* and *Wow! My baby moved today! It feels funny, like tickling from the inside out.* Suddenly I don't want to share anything else. My sister's comments seem too intimate. "We'll talk about it later." I tuck the booklet into the band of my jeans and begin making my sister's bed.

"Why are you doing that?"

I'm not sure myself. "Neatness factor," I finally say. Yet it does seem stupid. Why make a bed for someone who will never lie in it again?

By November, the mountains turn cold and all the autumn leaves have fallen off the trees. They look naked and hunkered down for the coming winter. The grass turns a dry, dull shade of brown. In Duncanville the annual craft fair is over and the stores are decorated for both Thanksgiving and Christmas at the same time. *Thanksmas,* Stu calls it. Our band is preparing for the huge Christmas tree sale we hold every year to raise funds for new uniforms, and everyone is asked to sign up for shifts as Santa's helpers—parents, kids, anyone who can move. The lot is set up next to the gym and the trees are shipped in from Canada. "Extra credit!" Mr. Mendoza says.

Christmas trees are scheduled to begin arriving Thanksgiving week, and when the sign-up sheet is passed around, I see that Stu has written his name next to every Saturday-afternoon slot until Christmas. I know for a fact that Melody has dance classes on Saturday afternoons, so that means Stu and I can work together without her. With my heart thumping, and feeling guilty for not wanting my best friend with us, I hastily write my name below his. I haven't been alone with him in *forever,* and I want to be. Despite all I'm going through, I can't get my feelings for him totally out of my head. He still makes my pulse jump and my insides go squirmy when I look in his eyes.

Mom and I visit the hospital once during the week and again on Sundays.

"You don't have to come, Sissy," Mom tells me the first time she prepares to go.

The school bus has dropped me off, and I've walked up our dirt driveway from the highway. "I want to come." I quickly hang my backpack on the newel post of the staircase.

"It's not like she'll know we're there," Mom says.

"After the baby's born, I won't see her again, will I?"

"No."

"Then I want to come with you every single time you go." It isn't as if I can go by myself. For the umpteenth time, I wish I was old enough to drive by myself.

Mom ties a scarf around her neck and tucks the ends into the neckline of her old wool jacket. "If that's what you want to do, okay. I've never tried to cushion you from the hard things in life, Sissy, and you've seen your share of hard things. I just want you to know that you have a choice about this one."

I can't explain to her that the baby brought Bree and me closer. We talked more than ever before while reading books about the upcoming birth. I found a stash of our old read-aloud books in the attic, and we dusted them off and laughed like crazy over the silly rhymes and goofy pictures. Bree was grateful because I painted the nursery, and because I played my flute over her tummy, and rubbed her feet when they hurt after she'd stood all day long. The past few months have closed the age gap between us. I can't leave her now. I have no choice at all.

At the hospital, Dr. Franklin has decided to keep Bree in Neuro ICU because visitors are allowed almost round the clock. True to his word, the tube connecting Bree to the breathing machine has been removed from her mouth and placed in a hole cut into her throat. She lies flat on the bed, her eyes half closed, her skin as smooth as vanilla pudding. "She looks so peaceful," Mom said the first time we saw her like that.

I touch Bree's arm. The IV has been removed and a feeding tube inserted so that her baby can be nourished with food and vitamins. Light from the wall beside her bed casts an eerie glow on her pale skin. Her wild hair has been smoothed away from her face and tied back with a red ribbon. I wonder who did that for her.

With the bed and the ventilator and the machines and wires hooked to electrodes monitoring the baby, it's a tight fit inside Bree's cubicle.

Mom and I stand across from each other with the hissing sounds of the vent squeezing out all other noise. In the large outer room, the nursing staff works. The beds fill and empty routinely as patients pass through. Doctors and lab technicians appear and disappear like smoke. It's like watching time-lapse photography through the clear glass walls when we visit. Healing is happening all around us, except in this cubicle. In here, my sister lies dead. But within her body, she shelters life, a being that still cannot survive outside her body without a hard-fought struggle and extraordinary medical intervention. In here, my mother and I watch and wait for a child to be born.

# EIGHT

Melody's mother invites Mom and me to join their family, Stu's family, plus assorted in-laws and cousins for Thanksgiving dinner. This beats our recent Thanksgivings every which way. The Thanksgiving feast was Grandma's favorite holiday and Bree and I would help her cook, but since her death it's all changed. Mom roasts a small turkey—a chicken one year—mashes some potatoes, warms some rolls, opens a can of cranberry sauce and presto! Thanksgiving dinner is served. When I see what Melody's mom and relatives lay out, I miss the old days even more.

Melody, Stu, a cousin and I sit at one of five smaller tables, while Mom and the other adults home in on the main table. No one asks about Briana, which is a relief because I couldn't talk about it without crying. The only time my sister is brought up is when Melody's father offers me and Mom a ride to the hospital anytime we want to go and don't want to drive. He works in the city and says he'll be glad to drop us off and bring us home after five. I can't imagine hanging around the hospital all day with nothing to do except listen to my sister's machine breathe for her.

All day I sneak peeks at Stu, who looks pretty hot in jeans and a sweater the same color as his eyes. He winks at me once and sends my pulse racing like a car engine, but he treats me as he always has—like a friend. He has no idea what I'm feeling toward him, and I'm sure not going to tell him!

After we clear the tables, Melody sets up a game of Monopoly and all of us play a cutthroat match. I'm almost bankrupt when a call goes out for an impromptu football game in the backyard. Everyone except Mom and the smallest cousins play. It's mass confusion, but my big moment comes when I get a handoff from Stu and wiggle my way through the other team to score a touchdown. "That's my girl!" Stu says, slapping me on the back. If he only knew how much I'd like to be his girl.

When it's time to leave, as casually as possible, I say to him, "See you at the tree sale on Saturday?"

"I'll be there," he tells me.

Melody flashes us a look I can't read, but then smiles. "Maybe I'll stop by after dance class."

"Great," Stu says with a matching smile.

"Yeah, great," I say, feeling a prick of disappointment. Like it or not, we'll be a threesome again on Saturday.

I don't know what wakes me tonight, but I sit upright with a start. My clock radio glows 4:00 a.m. I was planning on getting up at five anyway, because Melody and her mom are picking me up so we can hit the big mall in Chattanooga. We've done this ever since Melody and I turned ten and I always look forward to it. This year it doesn't matter much to me at all. I can hardly think about Christmas gifts and shopping, but Melody has made me promise to come with them, despite what's happened to Bree.

As I burrow in my bed, a sound floats up from the backyard through the silence. I hear the creaking of our old glider. Grandma liked sitting on it and watching the sun come up. *Maybe it's Grandma's ghost,* I think, then shake off sleep and go to the window to investigate. I see the silhouette of someone on the old rusty glider wrapped in a blanket, and go wide awake. I realize it's Mom, not Grandma, and alarmed, I throw on my sweats, a jacket and boots, grab my own blanket and hurry out into the cold, crisp air. I suck in my breath as the sharp chill hits my face.

"Mom? What are you doing out here? Are you all right? Did the hospital call about Bree?"

"No, nothing's changed for Bree. I couldn't sleep, Sissy." Her hands are wrapped around a coffee mug. "Come. Sit." She scoots over and I sit, tightening my blanket and shivering. "Did I wake you?" she asks.

"No. I have to get up soon anyway. Shopping, you know."

"I laid out some money for you on the hall

table." Mom resumes rocking the glider. "I'm not looking forward to the holidays. They'll be hard to get through this year."

"I don't need to go shopping today."

She pats my leg, which is covered with the blanket. "That's not what I mean. I'm trying to figure how best to pull it off. Tree? No tree? I had thought——" She stops herself, takes a deep breath. "We're going to miss your sister."

Her voice wavers and a lump pushes into my throat. "She was gone last Christmas too," I remind her, because I don't want her to be too sad.

"We didn't know where she was. But we did know she was alive," Mom reminds me. She tilts her head to look up at the stars still glittering in the sky. "Bree always was my wild and crazy child. She couldn't wait to grow up. Had to have everything *right now*. No matter how hard I sat on her, she just went her own way."

Mom isn't really talking to me, just saying her mind out loud. I don't interrupt. Once she goes quiet, I say, "The way the doctor explained it, what happened to Bree could have happened anytime. It wasn't your fault . . . the thing in her head. It just *blew up*."

"I know that in my head. But in my heart . . ." I hear Mom sniff. "It's too cold to be sitting out here."

Neither of us moves.

"I sure loved that girl, Sissy. She made me crazy, but I loved her."

"You two fought a lot." It isn't a criticism, but an observation.

"Yes, we did. I wanted so much for her to have a good life. It's what parents want, you know . . . for their kids to have good lives."

Bree made some poor choices, but I don't state the obvious. "We'll love her baby too, Mom."

Mom sighs. "Lots of work raising a child." Before I can comment, she asks, "Bree ever tell you if she picked a name for the baby? The baby should have a name, you know."

I asked my sister the same thing. "You can't give a name to someone you've never looked at," Bree answered. "A person needs to look like the name you give them. Know what I mean? What if I picked out a name and got my mind settled on it, and then when she's born and I take a long look at her, I see that she doesn't look like that name at all? I'd have to change it on the spot. So I think it's best to wait until she's born, then figure out a name. And that's what I'm going to do."

I tell Mom what Bree said.

Bemused, Mom bobs her head. "Crazy girl. That baby has no father, no mother, no name. I guess it'll be up to us, won't it, Sissy?"

"I guess so."

"Well, you think on it. We've got to put something down on her birth certificate."

"We'll figure out a good name for her, Mom."

"Briana." Mom speaks my sister's name into the dark. "Do you know what it means, Sissy?"

I say I don't.

"It means 'strong.' And she was strong-willed, that's for sure."

"What does my name mean?"

"*Lily.* From the Hebrew. A sweet, beautiful flower. You're well named." She strokes my hair and I lean against her blanket-covered shoulder and together we cry.

I can't get into shopping. The stores are crowded, lots of pushing and shoving over 'on sale' and 'today only' stuff. Christmas music blares every place we go, and because our band has been practicing most of the same music since October, I'm sick of it. I don't let on to Melody or her mom how bad I'm feeling, though. I just paste a smile on my face and trail around after them, oohing and aahing over everything they like, wrinkling my nose over the stuff they don't.

I buy Mom a soft-as-silk fleece neck scarf and matching gloves. In the bookstore, I buy Stu a book about Winston Churchill and for me, a baby-naming book.

Melody grabs it out of my hands and flips through the pages. "This is cool! Are you looking for a special name?"

"It's for the baby. Mom told me to pick one out for her."

"I'd love to help you choose a name!"

"Um . . . I think Mom wants a shot at it first. I mean, since she's the grandmother and all." Telling that little lie doesn't bother me one bit. Melody can be pushy at times.

She looks up her own name. "*Melody:* 'song.' Well, duh! No surprise there." She flips over to another section and reads, "*Stuart:* 'caretaker.'" She giggles. "Should we tell him?"

I carefully extract the book from her hands. "Why not keep it our little secret? It might go to his head."

Distracted, Melody quickly forgets about the book and I slip it back into the store bag with its receipt.

When we stop to eat a late lunch, Melody's mother eyes our shopping bags. "You only have two bags, Susanna. We're way ahead of you."

I nibble on a rubbery-tasting egg salad sandwich. "Small shopping list this year," I say.

She looks stricken and her face grows pink. "What's the matter with me? Honey, I'm very sorry. How could I be so insensitive?"

I'm embarrassed because I didn't mean to make her feel bad. "I—it's okay. Really."

She pats the table with her palm. "You know what? As soon as we finish eating we're going into that baby store on the second level. We need to buy that baby some pretty clothes."

And that's what we do. Melody's mother chooses outfits in three different infant sizes. "So she'll have something to grow into," she tells me. She tosses a green velvet baby dress with red ribbons onto the stack. It looks very Christmasy.

"She won't be born until January," I remind her.

"No matter. We'll buy it for next Christmas." She finds a larger size.

Melody picks out a cute baby hat and tiny socks. I find a soft blanket with pale purple giraffes, trimmed in lime green—the same colors as the nursery.

I feel better after our side shopping trip. I can't buy a gift for my sister this year, but I can buy gifts for her baby.

When we pile into the car for the trip home, Melody's mother turns to me and quietly asks, "Would you like to stop at the hospital, Susanna? Mellie and I can wait in the lobby while you run up and see Briana."

I feel as if she's read my mind. "Would you mind? Would it be all right?"

"Absolutely," she says.

I could kiss her.


"I won't stay long," I promise before heading to the elevator.

"Take all the time you need," Melody's mother says.

"Are you sure we can't come with you?" Melody asks.

"Only family's allowed," I say, glad of the policy. I don't want anyone gawking at my sister, not even my best friend.

I ride up to Neuro ICU, push through the double doors. The nurses at the desk wave to me. They know Mom and me by now. I walk to Briana's cubicle and see a woman leaning over her. My heart freezes. "What are you doing to my sister?" I ask.

# NINE

The woman turns, flashes me a smile. "I'm Nicole, your sister's physical therapist. You must be Susanna. The nurses told me about you."

I'm speechless. *Physical therapy for someone who's technically dead?* Doesn't she know about Bree?

Nicole says, "Come closer. I'll show you what I'm doing." Warily I shuffle to the bed. The covers have been thrown back and the hospital gown barely covers Bree's thin legs. "See how her hands and legs are drawing up?"

My sister has only been lying here for a couple of weeks, but already I see a difference. Her hands are turning toward her wrists and her fingers are beginning to look clawlike. Her legs are pulling closer to her body.

"It's called contracturing. Muscles begin to shrink from inactivity and that causes the limbs to curl. I come in and massage and manipulate a patient's joints to keep that from happening. I also turn the patient several times a day so bedsores won't form. Bedsores are caused from lying in the same position day after day. It helps keep a patient comfortable."

"But Bree—"

"I know her condition." Nicole interrupts me kindly. "But a bedsore can cause an infection that can get into her bloodstream and cross over to her baby."

I watch for a few minutes as Nicole gently kneads Bree's arms and legs, stretching and rubbing the joints. My sister looks like a mannequin, a life-sized doll whose body lies at odd angles. I can't stand to watch another minute. I back out of the cubicle and leave the unit, hit the stairwell door at the end of the hall, and hurtle down eleven flights of stairs, crying every step of the way.

• • •

On Saturday, I change outfits five times before leaving for the Christmas tree lot at school. "Sissy, I have an appointment with a client and I'm going to be late if you don't hurry!" Mom calls from the foot of the stairs.

"I'm hurrying," I shout, ripping off a sweater, knowing it's too fancy for a day around tree sap. I jerk on an old sweatshirt, grab my work gloves and a hoodie and rush downstairs. *Who am I kidding? Stu won't notice unless I show up naked.*

"Susanna! Thank goodness you're here," Mr. Mendoza calls as I get out of Mom's car in the crowded parking lot. "You and Stuart are the only ones who've shown up so far. Patsy and Nolan and a couple of dads are coming later, but we need help *now.*"

The trees have been set up in rows by type, tied to stakes hammered into the ground. Half the town appears to be wandering through the lot, fingering branches, each in a quest for the perfect tree. "What should I do?"

"Go help Stu unload the truck that came in last night. It's around back."

I wave to Mrs. Mendoza, who is wearing a money apron, and hurry around the side of the gym, where a huge semitruck, its back doors wide open, sits in the cold sunlight. I climb the ramp into the truck and discover Stu wrestling with piles of bundled trees, stacked in mounds like cordwood. The scent of fresh evergreens is overpowering. "Hey," I say. "The cavalry's here."

He looks up, red-faced with exertion. "Pretty small army you're leading."

"Do you want help, or not?"

He wipes his forehead, walks over and squeezes my upper arm. "Seems strong enough."

"Ha, ha," I say, warm all over from his touch. "What's the plan?"

"You pick up the top of the tree; I'll lift from the base. We carry it outside, cut the strings, stand it up and shake it out good. Tons of loose needles in them, and Mendoza said the trees have to look fresh if people are going to buy them. Once outside, we'll lean the trees against the wall."

"Is that all?"

"Until help arrives. You know . . . the rest of your cavalry. They can carry the trees to the lot and stake them. It's a harder job. Serves them right for being late."

We start working and in an hour have freed

and shaken more than forty-five trees. Lined up against the back wall of the gym, they look like a dark green forest. At some point help arrives and Stu and I take a break inside the gym on the basketball court. We fish sodas out of a cooler reserved for us workers.

"You sure you don't want hot chocolate?" he asks. Pots full of hot water and packets of cocoa and coffee are also available.

"I'm sweating," I tell him, then regret my self-description. How alluring must *that* sound!

We climb midway up the bleachers, sit and pop open our sodas.

"You doing all right?" he asks.

"The front ends of the trees aren't very heavy, you know. I can handle the job."

"That's not what I'm asking about." He grows quiet and I stare into his eyes. A girl can drown in his eyes. Suddenly realizing that he isn't asking about my stamina, I gulp from my soda can. He's asking me about Briana.

"I'm doing just fine. Honest."

"You never talk about her. Not to me. Not to Melody either."

"It's not something I like talking about."

"But we're your friends. In the beginning, you told us plenty."

I shrug. "Not much to say anymore. The doctors are just waiting for the baby to get big enough to be born." I don't add, *And for Bree to die,* but that will happen too.

"Melody says you're in charge of naming the baby. That you bought a book."

"I'm just looking up different names and their meanings. We won't name her until she's born. Until we see her and all."

"Melody says you've already bought the baby some clothes."

"Is that all you and Melody do? Sit around and talk about my life?"

My outburst startles him. "No way. And you don't have to go postal. I'm just trying to be a friend."

I hang my head. "Sorry," I say.

He reaches over, puts his hand on my shoulder. "We worry about you. I think about you a lot."

"You do?"

His eyes look like deep pools of blue water. My heart thuds like a jackhammer.

"There you two are! I've been looking all over for you."

Melody's voice saves me from drowning.

Stu drops his hand from my shoulder, waves her up to where we're sitting. "Break time."

She climbs up, eyes us suspiciously. I stand, my insides quivering. "Back to work," I say. "How was dance?"

"Same-same. How are tree sales?"

"We have enough for Mendoza to buy himself a new baton and a whistle," Stu jokes.

Melody breaks into laughter. I only smile. Stu's stab at humor isn't *that* funny. I precede them outside, glad for the sharp slap of cold on my face. I go over the conversation I've had with Stu. He said he was worried about me. He said he thought about me. *A lot!* Do we have a chance to be more than friends? If only Melody hadn't barged in when she did. Something will have to change drastically if I'm ever going to be more than just friends with Stu. And that something does *not* include Melody.

On most days my brain is a bouncing ball. My thoughts flash from Briana to her nameless baby, from Stu to Melody, from me-Melody-Stu to schoolwork, from band practice to the coming holidays. I start to think about one thing but before I can concentrate on how to deal with it, my brain cells jump to something else and I end up not figuring out anything about *anything*. I hate rubber-ball thinking!

Mom's really busy closing out year-end books for different clients, so she's barricaded in her office for long hours. I've practiced my solo parts for our holiday show so much that I can perform them in my sleep, and I finish homework assignments ahead of schedule. I have time to myself, and I spend much of it in Bree's bedroom. I don't know why I feel better sitting in her room, but I do. I've neatened it up, put things into place, vacuumed and dusted, although I know she's never coming back to stay here again. The only thing I don't do is wash her bedding. The pillow still holds her scent and I press my face into it, close my eyes and imagine she's still alive.

I've always looked up to her. Growing up, she was too busy to pay me much attention, but I never minded. I *liked* her, thought she was cool. I didn't argue with Mom like Bree did. I guess I never liked yelling or being yelled at. Bree must have thought it was her duty to make up for my lack of spirit. Mom made rules Bree refused to follow——Mom called it damage control——but when Bree was around, life was never dull.

I go back to my earliest and most vivid memory of my sister. Daddy has died and Mom is packing up our old house for the move to Tennessee. I'm sitting on the porch steps, my face buried in my hands, crying. Mom has told me to sit down and stay out of the way. I've been sitting there and crying forever when Bree comes over and gives me a tissue. "What's the problem, Sissy?"

"I miss Daddy," I say.

She looks sad. "I miss him too."

"What if Daddy comes home and we're gone?" I obviously haven't gotten the death angle straight in my head. "What if he can't find us?"

"He's not coming home."

"But why? Did I do something wrong?"

"Don't you remember the funeral, Sissy?" I nod. "The man in the box was Daddy."

The man in the box hadn't looked a thing like my father to me. My daddy smiled a lot. The man in the box never moved. "I only looked once," I confess. I remember shutting my eyes tight right after Mom led me to the casket and told me to tell Daddy goodbye.

"Remember how we rode in the big car to the cemetery? Remember how they buried the box in the hole in the ground?"

"But the pastor said Daddy was sleeping." I hear the pastor's words exactly . . . my daddy was "asleep and will one day rise up." I remind Bree what the pastor said. "So what if he wakes up and wants to come home, and when he gets here, we're gone?"

Bree puts her arm around my shoulders. "The preacher didn't mean it that way."

"Then why did he say it?"

"It's just his way of talking about Daddy being in heaven."

"So Daddy's not coming back?" I cry some more. Bree is almost nine, so I take her word for it, but I just can't wrap my mind around never seeing our dad again.

She thinks for a minute. "I have an idea. Go get a piece of paper, and I'll write down Grandma's address, and you can put it in our mailbox. That way, he'll know where to come and find us."

I run into the house, find a piece of scrap paper and take it to Bree. I watch her carefully write numbers and letters on it. She hands it to me. "There you go."

I grab it, fold it, dash to the curbside mailbox and tuck it inside. I feel so much better knowing we've left Daddy a message. I skip back to the porch and hug Bree hard.

Bree unwinds my arms from her neck. "You know, Sissy, don't get your hopes up. I don't believe people are allowed to check out of heaven once they get there."

I remember her words all these years later. By the time we have settled in with Grandma in Tennessee and I've started first grade, I've stopped expecting Dad to show up. People don't return from the dead. Not then. Not now.

# ⓉⒺⓃ

The next time I see my sister, Dr. Kendrow is leaning over her bed. She smiles at me as I come into the cubicle. "Hello, Susanna. Remember me?"

"You're the baby's doctor."

"I will be once she's born," she says. "Is your mother with you?"

"She stopped in the cafeteria to get coffee, but I didn't want to wait."

Dr. Kendrow pulls the earpieces of her stethoscope from her ears. "I was listening to the baby's heartbeat."

"I thought that machine kept tabs on the

baby's heart." I point to a machine with wires that snake under the bedcovers. I know the wires are attached to Bree's abdomen.

"It does, but I listen anyway. Would you like to hear the baby's heart?"

"Well . . . sure. Can I?"

She places the stethoscope's earpieces in my ears and the flat part against Bree's taut skin. "It's a whooshing sound. Listen closely."

I have to concentrate hard, but then I hear it—a soft swishing sound, slight and rapid. It makes me smile. Then I worry. "Is it supposed to beat so fast?"

"Oh yes. Babies' heartbeats are much faster than ours. It's a strong one too. I like what I'm hearing."

"Is she ready to be born?" The idea makes *my* heart beat faster.

"Not yet. Another six weeks or so. Babies gain a lot of their birth weight in their last month. And her lungs aren't fully developed either. We don't want her to have breathing issues."

*Issues.* The word sounds odd. How can a newborn baby have issues? "I know about the layer of cells in the lungs that get a baby ready to breathe air." I hand back the stethoscope and Dr. Kendrow tucks it into her lab coat's pocket.

"You do? How so?"

"I have a book. It was Bree's. It tells all about how babies develop inside the mother. I . . . um . . . like following along."

"Good for you. I was pretty curious myself when I was younger. I drove my parents crazy asking *why* all the time." She studies me for a minute. "Does your book tell you that a baby can hear in the womb?"

"Bree read that to me, and that's when I started playing my flute for her baby. I'm in the school band, and I like playing. I was going to play for her every day. But . . . but then . . ." I don't finish my thought.

"If you want to bring your flute and play for her here in the hospital, you can," Dr. Kendrow says.

"Really?"

"I'll clear it with the nurses out there." She gestures toward the outer room. "You can talk to the baby too, Susanna. So can your mother. Get her used to your voices. Babies can and will respond to familiar voices."

"Like how?"

"They wiggle around inside the womb, or quiet down at the sound of voices they recognize."

"My book says that they have hair and that they can blink by week thirty-four. Is that true?"

"All true."

"I guess babies are pretty smart, even before they're born."

Dr. Kendrow grins at me. "This is a lucky little baby to have an aunt as caring as you."

That makes me self-conscious. "I can't wait to hold her."

"Just another month or so and you will be holding her, if—"

"If what?"

"If she can stay put," the doctor finishes, a look on her face that tells me she wishes she hadn't added the *if* to her sentence. "Her best chance for a healthy beginning is staying in your sister's womb until it's time to be born."

"How will you know when it's time?"

"Tests. We do plenty of tests, you know. And sometimes labor just starts."

I start to ask, *And what if she doesn't stay in Bree's womb?* But then I decide that sometimes it's best not to ask too many questions. I don't want one more thing to worry about either. Just then Mom comes into the cubicle, and she and Dr. Kendrow talk. I tune them out and instead watch as dual green squiggly lines shoot up and down on the screens of the machines beside Bree's bed—both reflections of human heart-beats, mother's and daughter's.

The very next time I come to visit, I bring my flute. I wedge a chair between the machines, lean close to Bree's abdomen and play softly, hoping the baby can hear it. It's weird, sitting in a cubicle playing for an audience of one who can't see me and doesn't even know me. The nurses at the desk peek in several times. One of them, Cynthia, asks, "Can we make requests?"

"Sure. If I know the music, I'll play it."

She suggests a few Christmas carols, comes over and straightens Bree's covers. "May I say something to you, Susanna?" I lower my flute. "All of us nurses think you're a pretty special girl."

"Me?"

"Not many kids your age would spend so much time up here voluntarily."

"But we're sisters."

Cynthia nods. "Some of our patients have big

families, but not all of them can handle knowing that their loved one is never going to be the way he or she used to be. It's hard to accept that someone you love will spend a lifetime as a quadriplegic."

I wish Bree *could be* a quadriplegic; at least then she'd be alive. But I also know she would have hated that kind of life. "It's not fair," I say.

"Life's never fair," Cynthia says. "Still, it's what we have to work with, isn't it?" She leaves the cubicle. I pick up my flute and play "What Child Is This?", a song she has requested. It's about Mary holding a sleeping baby Jesus on her lap while angels sing—something Bree will never get to do.

The signs and symbols of Christmas are everywhere. Lightposts in downtown Duncanville have been dressed up with fake holly and big red bows. The store windows are lit with blinking colored lights and splashed with glitter. The large fir tree in the courthouse square is decorated with king-sized ornaments and an ocean of lights. At school, the official bulletin board has been trimmed with cutouts of Santa's elves and long strings draped with holiday cards.

In the middle of the hospital lobby, there's a tree decorated with paper angel tags that show the names of children and elderly people who are especially needy. People are urged to take an angel and help give that person a happier Christmas or Chanukah. In the intensive care unit, cutouts of turkeys and pilgrims have been replaced with ones of wreaths, menorahs and gift packages. A tiny artificial tree is perched on the corner of the central desk and hung with ornaments made from medical supplies—latex gloves, empty injection barrels, a surgical mask, empty test tubes and pill bottles.

Christmas is everywhere. Except at our house. Mom asks me, "Do you mind if we don't decorate this year?"

We have an old artificial tree that's hard to assemble, but I do it every year. Then Mom and I throw on some lights, ornaments and tinsel. Last year I tried squirting on artificial snow, but the stuff gave me an allergy attack. "I'll go to Melody's if I want to look at a tree," I tell Mom, disappointed. She looks relieved.

I place a few candy dishes around the living room and fill them with Christmas candy from

Wal-Mart. I also put my pots of Christmas cactuses on a red velvet placemat on the coffee table. Amazingly, the plants are still alive, and full of buds. I'm feeling pretty good about my efforts, but when Stu and Melody drop by, Stu says, "Whoa! No Christmas this year? I'm Jewish and we decorate more than this."

"Mom's not in the mood," I say, my feelings hurt. "And where is it written that we have to decorate for Christmas anyway? Who cares?"

Melody asks, "Where will you stack your presents?"

Doesn't she get it? Mom and I aren't doing Christmas this year.

"I know." Melody doesn't wait for me to answer. "You can put them in front of the fireplace. On the brick. That would be pretty."

"Won't Santa trip over them when he comes down the chimney?" Stu jokes. "Do you want Santa to sue you?"

"The fat boy's on his own," I snap back.

"We can help you decorate if you want," Melody offers.

"What part of 'not this year' do you two not understand?"

They glance at each other; then Stu sends me a sidelong look. "Sorry. I didn't mean for it to sound like a critique. I was just trying to make you smile."

Not much amuses me these days, but I shrug, implying that I'm okay and all's forgiven.

"I brought a DVD to watch," Melody says, changing the subject. She scoops a thin box from her purse. "A holiday comedy," she says. "Want to watch it with us?"

"Sure," I lie. I'm feeling contrite about getting angry at them. "I'll get some popcorn going."

Stu reaches into a sack he's carried inside. "Popcorn and sodas are on me. This is a full-service cinema experience. You get to sit. We know the way to your microwave."

They head for the kitchen and I settle on the sofa, my feelings in flux. They're trying to make us a threesome again, as tight and carefree as we were in the old days. Except that everything is different now. Not just with what has happened to Bree, but for what's happening between the three of us. My feelings for Stu have not gone away like I'd hoped. And my friendship with Melody isn't the same anymore either. I feel caught in some mysterious current that's moving me along a stream I can't control. I'm a leaf adrift on a winter current that will not let me go.

The holiday break and our final concert are only days away. The band is in the auditorium and in the middle of a huge dress rehearsal with the elementary kids from first through fifth grades. The kids are all talking at once and teachers are trying to restore order when Melody nudges me and asks, "Isn't that your mother in the back?"

Sure enough, Mom is hurrying down a side aisle toward the stage. I go cold. She never comes to school to see me unless . . . I set my flute on my chair and rush down the steps of the stage to meet her. I almost trip over a pack of second graders being herded into place. "What's wrong?" I see by her expression that *something* is wrong.

"Get your things. The hospital called. Ready or not, Bree's baby is coming."

# ELEVEN

"What happened?" I ask once we're in the car. My whole body is shaking.

"Dr. Kendrow called and said the baby's heartbeat was slowing and so they were taking Bree up to Maternity for an immediate C-section."

I rapidly count the number of weeks until January fourteenth, Bree's estimated due date. There are six. "B-but it's too soon."

"The doctors know what they're doing. They have to do what's best for the baby." The bulging joints of Mom's arthritic hands look clenched and pale on the steering wheel, like the bones might poke through her skin.

"The baby was doing just fine yesterday," I

say. "What went wrong?" I ask the question in spite of seeing that Mom is losing patience with me. I don't know why I ask dumb questions when I'm scared, but I do.

"Be quiet, Sissy," Mom says. "I don't know anything more than what I've already told you."

We arrive at the hospital and go straight to the maternity floor, only to be told that Dr. Kendrow wants us to wait for her inside a tiny cubicle off one of the hallways. "How's the baby?" Mom asks.

The nurse says, "She's been taken to Neonatal ICU."

"But is she too premature?"

"The doctor will be here any minute," the nurse says sympathetically.

Minutes later, Dr. Kendrow shows up and drags a chair close to me and Mom. The doctor is wearing green scrubs and a surgical hat. By now I feel sick to my stomach and I'm hoping I don't throw up. She says quickly, "The baby is fine. We have her in an oxygen mask and a special incubator in ICU. I'm thinking she's about thirty-four, maybe thirty-five weeks old. That's good. She's seventeen and a half inches long, four and three-quarters pounds."

Mom asks, "And her lungs?"

"She'll need a little help breathing for a while."

"Can we see her?" I blurt out.

"In a minute," Dr. Kendrow says. I can tell she has something else on her mind that she wants to tell us.

Mom asks, "What happened? Why was the baby in trouble?"

The doctor takes her time answering. "Briana came down with a sudden and fast-moving infection and we thought it best to get the baby out quickly."

"And my daughter?"

"Briana's heart stopped about noon and we could no longer sustain her on life support."

A hammer hits my chest. Tears fill my eyes. My sister has been dead all along, but now the machines are gone and with them our illusion of life.

Mom bows her head. "I—I . . ."

Dr. Kendrow reaches out and clasps Mom's hands, clenched together in her lap. "I'm so very sorry. I wish things could have gone differently." Dr. Kendrow still doesn't move. I can't believe there's anything left for her to say, but there is.

"Before I take you in to see the baby, I thought you might like some time alone with your daughter. She's in the delivery room."

Mom nods, reaches over and takes my hand. "You coming, Sissy?"

My throat is clogged. I stand up on wobbly legs. An hour ago, I was playing my flute; now I'm telling Bree goodbye forever.

We follow Dr. Kendrow through doors marked AUTHORIZED PERSONNEL ONLY.

The surgical room is small, with all kinds of equipment and big silver overhead lights that are turned off and no longer shining on the table below them. The room is icy cold, and my teeth chatter. Bree lies on the table, covered by clean sheets pulled up to her neck. Holding hands, Mom and I walk over, look down on Bree's pretty face. She looks serene, her skin smooth as glass.

Her arms and legs make straight lines beneath the sheet, no longer drawing up as when she was on life support. I wonder if Nicole has come down and straightened them out, then realize that someone else has probably done this.

"Hello, honey." Mom touches my sister's cheek.

I want to touch her too, but I don't. I tell myself there's no difference between this version of Bree and the one who has lain up in the Neuro unit, but I press my palms against my thighs, unable to reach out and do it.

"Take all the time you want." Dr. Kendrow's voice startles me. I've forgotten she's with us.

Mom's crying hard now. I cry more quietly. *We'll take good care of your baby,* I pledge to my sister in my heart.

"What happens to Bree now?" Mom asks.

"Call the mortuary. They'll help you handle every detail."

It strikes me like a blow that now we must face Bree's funeral and bury her in Duncanville, next to Grandma, in the old cemetery on the hill. Once, when we were younger and were driving past it, Stu pointed at the headstones sprinkled over the green grass and said, "People are dying to get in there!" And Melody and I laughed. *Laughed!* I glance at Mom.

"I've made some arrangements already," she says softly. This shocks me. *When?* I think. The words never reach my mouth. I am mute. Dumbstruck. Mom turns to me. "I bought her a pale pink casket with white satin lining. Do you think she'll like that?"

She speaks as if Bree might veto the choice. The picture in my head of my sister in a casket is chilling. *Bree . . . pretty in pink.*

Mom strokes Bree's arm down the length of the top sheet. "I love you, little girl." She steps backward and so do I. I don't think I can stand there one more minute without screaming. "We're ready to leave," Mom says.

Dr. Kendrow leads us out. Just before we step through the door, I look up and see that someone has hung a long sprig of mistletoe from the doorjamb. I think, *Kiss it all goodbye.* Then the doors close behind us with a whoosh and we leave the room holding death and head down the hall toward the room holding life.

Neonatal ICU is brightly lit, brimming with color. Nurses are dressed in pale blue slacks and tops printed with teddy bears, baby bunnies, kittens and puppies. Incubators line walls and look like transparent eggshells with babies inside lying bundled in blankets, small packages awaiting home delivery.

"This way," Dr. Kendrow says, and we follow her to an incubator near the front of the unit.

My heart's beating fast as I peer inside the thick plastic shell. A tiny, perfectly formed human being lies on a clean sheet, naked except for a diaper about the size of a single square of toilet paper. A mask covers half her face, and cotton balls are taped across her eyes.

"To protect her eyes from the lights," Dr. Kendrow says. "She was born a little jaundiced; many newborns are. It disappears after a few days under this special light."

Bree's baby is doll-sized. I watch the rapid movement of her chest. It reminds me of hummingbird wings hovering over the red feeder outside our kitchen window. Electrodes are taped to the baby's upper body, and wires lead to a machine beside the incubator. I watch the quick, steady movement of the green light on the screen representing her beating heart. I remember the green line on the machine beside Bree's bed. That was a machine-generated line. This one is not.

I search for my sister's image on what I can see of the baby's face. Mom is the first one to recognize Bree's genes because she says, "Briana had a full head of black hair when she was born too."

I feel relief. This really is my sister's baby. "Can I hold her?" I ask.

"Not yet," the doctor says. "But clean your hands with these wipes and you can touch her." She gives us each a foil-wrapped disinfectant cloth.

I scrub my palms and fingertips hard.

Dr. Kendrow raises the lid. I rub my hand lightly down the baby's skinny leg, still curled from being crammed inside Bree's body. Her foot is the size of my thumb and her skin is soft as powder.

Mom's hands are such a contrast to the baby's satiny skin that it takes my breath. I realize how deformed her disease has made her joints, and it makes me sad. We both withdraw our hands and Dr. Kendrow lowers the lid. "You can come visit her anytime day or night."

A card is taped to the outside of the incubator with a pink stork stamped on it. It reads: SCANLAND, GIRL. For some reason, this surprises me. The baby has been recorded, her

existence written down. What has lain so long a
mystery inside my sister is now a fact, made
more real by our family name affixed to a card.

Dr. Kendrow asks, "Have you chosen a
name yet?"

Mom glances at me. "That's Susanna's job."

But the doctor already knows this. I fidget,
recalling a list of names from the baby-naming
book that I've scribbled down. The choices rip
through my head. None seems to fit the baby.
"Well . . . I—I . . . not yet," I mumble. Dr.
Kendrow probably thinks I'm stupid. How hard
is it to choose a name?

"There's plenty of time for that," the doctor
says. "She's going to be here for a few weeks."

"Any idea how long?" Mom asks.

"Until her lungs are fully developed. We'd
like her to weigh about five pounds too. She'll
lose some of her birth weight at first, so it might
not be until after the first of the year before she
goes home."

*Lose some weight!* Is she kidding? I can't imagine the baby any smaller. As soon as school is out
for the holidays, I vow to be here every day and
watch over her. That's all I want. To stay and not
leave her.

"Just remember, she's been born too soon," the doctor goes on to say.

Is this some kind of warning?

"We have one of the top NICUs in the South, though," she continues, as if to reassure us. "She'll have the best care we can give her."

We say nothing, just stand and stare down at the infant inside the bubble.

"We should go," Mom says finally.

I start to protest, then remember why we have to leave. Briana is dead and must be buried. I close my eyes, trying to conjure up my sister's face. All I see is the baby. Small and fragile and fighting to learn how to breathe on her own.

# T W E L V E

I'm fourteen years old and this is the third time I've gone to a funeral home to do the visitation thing. That's when a person's casket is put into a room at a funeral home with lots of flowers, and people come from all over town to "pay their last respects." It's a hateful ritual. At my father's visitation, I peeked at him in his casket and cried because he wouldn't wake up. My tears didn't bring him back, but on the plus side, I didn't have to stay very long.

At Grandma's visitation, Bree and I hung with Mom four whole hours, except when Bree sneaked out back to smoke and have a make-out session with her boyfriend of the moment. I never told Mom this, even though I know it was wrong of Bree to do it. At the time, I wanted to get away from the place too. The smell of the flowers was getting to me, and people I didn't know kept asking me questions and trying to hug me—comfort me, they said.

This time is different. I'm still trapped in a room with a ton of flowers and my mother, but there's no sister to help me pass the time. Mom's holding the visitation on Saturday morning, to be followed by the funeral and burial. Bree's casket is open and people keep telling Mom she looks beautiful. I don't look at her in the casket at all.

I'm blown away by the number of people who show up. People who knew Bree from school. People she's worked with. People who hardly even knew her. I can't figure out why so many people show up.

I ask Mom and she says, "No one except you and I got to see her the whole time she was in the hospital. They knew she wasn't really alive that whole time, but they still need to tell her goodbye."

I wonder if anyone has told Jerry out in L.A., but decide I don't want him to know because I'm afraid he'll have a change of heart and come take his baby. She's ours now. Didn't he already tell Bree he didn't want the baby?

"Hey, Susanna."

I turn around and see Stuart dressed in a dark suit and a tie, and I realize I've never seen him dressed up before. He looks terrific. I feel my spirits rise just looking at him. "Where's Mellie?" I ask, because they often seem to appear together.

"She has that mandatory dance rehearsal. She had to go, but told me she'll call you later."

I've forgotten. Her big holiday ballet extravaganza is on Saturday night, following our Friday night holiday performance at the school. I'm supposed to go. "Oh yeah. Now I remember."

"Are you all right?"

"I guess."

"Can we go outside? I don't like it in here."

I see Mom across the room surrounded by clients of hers. "I can't stay long," I say, knowing the visitation ritual ends in a half hour.

He takes my elbow. I'm glad to leave the

building, but although the day is sunshiny, it's cold. I wrap my arms around my shoulders.

"We can sit in my parents' car," he says. "I know they'll be inside there for a while."

In the car, it's toasty warm and I lean my head back against the seat. "The baby's beautiful," I tell Stu, then wonder why I said it. He hasn't asked about the baby.

"Maybe Mellie and I can come up and see her over the holiday break."

"I'll ask the doctor." I want my friends to see her. I want them all to wish they had a tiny baby to love the way I do.

"I guess you won't be helping at the Christmas tree sale today."

I haven't given the sale and my promise to help a single thought.

"You don't have to. I know Mr. Mendoza will excuse you and I'll bet he lets you keep your extra credit too."

But I want to go. After Grandma's funeral, Mom wouldn't even let us watch TV. I was sad about Grandma, but I was bored too. Mom's already told me that lots of people will come by the house today after the graveside service.

Plus, she's said that we won't go back to the hospital to see the baby until tomorrow. "I'll bet Mom will let me come and help." I tell Stu how people will show up and stand around eating and talking. "Then they all leave and we're alone staring at the walls. I don't want to sit around doing nothing the rest of the day. I'll go crazy!" I look out the window and see the long black hearse at the side entrance of the funeral home. I know that soon they'll put Bree's casket inside and take it to the cemetery. Parked behind the hearse is the black limo for me and Mom. Last time, Bree was sitting in a limo with us. My family's dwindling, one by one, being taken to cemeteries right and left. I shudder just thinking about it.

"You do funerals different from our tradition," Stu says.

"How so?"

"After the funeral we sit shiva."

"What's shiva?"

"Remember when we were in the sixth grade and my grandfather died in New York?"

I remember.

"The family gathers together. We sat in the

house with my grandmother for a week after he was buried."

"Go on!"

Stu continues. "Honest. We sit shiva for all close family members."

"For a whole *week*?"

"If it's possible. Dad told me that the family does this because a person's spirit supposedly continues to dwell in the place where he lived. We even sleep at the house of the person who's died if there's enough space. If that's not possible, we leave after dark, but we have to be back in the morning. Family and friends bring food and we sit around together. People talk about good times. They share memories. It's supposed to help us grieve and realize the living have to go on with their lives."

I think about Bree's spirit, but I don't picture her spirit living in our house, because all she wanted was to run away and have exciting adventures. I tell Stu, "Bree's spirit lives in her baby."

I'm not going to cry at the cemetery. I've cried an ocean of tears already, and this time half the people in Duncanville are standing around watching and listening to the pastor saying words of farewell. I refuse to dissolve in front of them.

I stand next to Mom under a canopy. Everybody else is standing in the hot sun, I'll bet wishing that the pastor would hurry up and finish. Stu and his parents are off to one side. He catches my eye and winks, and I go all gooey inside. I shouldn't feel this way at my sister's funeral service, but then I recall how much Bree liked boys and I bet she'd get a laugh out of me drooling over a guy while so many other people are crying over her.

When it's finally over, I ask Mom if I can go to the school and the tree sale instead of the house. "You have your good clothes on," she says. Just like Mom to think about this first.

"I'll stand around and collect tree money," I tell her. "I won't get messed up. Promise."

She agrees—too overwhelmed to argue with me, I guess—and so I hitch a ride with Stu. Sitting in the backseat next to him feels wonderful, and I pretend his mom and dad aren't up front driving us and the circumstances are

different. At the school, Stu removes a duffel
bag from the trunk and after his parents drive
off, he says, "I'm going to the locker room to
change."

Mr. Mendoza and his wife come over and say
how sorry they are about Bree and that I didn't
have to come. I tell them it's all right, that I
need something to do to get my mind off the
funeral. Mrs. Mendoza insists on driving me
home after the lot closes tonight. I'd rather be
with Stu for the drive, but I know it isn't fair to
have his mother take me out to my place when
Stu only lives a few blocks from the school.

People are showing up to buy trees, so I get
busy. I recognize faces from the funeral, but
only a few people bring it up. With Christmas
closing in, most just want to buy a tree and
leave.

"Only fifteen days until Christmas," I hear a
woman say to her husband. Their two kids are
squabbling and pushing each other into the trees
we've anchored in such neat rows.

The dad roars, "Stop it or Santa won't come
this year." The little boy starts crying and his sister sticks out her tongue at him.

I get a lump in my throat because the scene seems like something from a TV show, so sitcom ordinary. A dark cloud descends on me and I feel like I'm going to shatter. I say "Excuse me" and take off, not wanting to break down in front of these strangers. I make it all the way across the football field before I fall apart. I duck under the bleachers and lean against a concrete wall. The bottom falls out and I can't stop the flood. I'm so into crying that I don't see Stu come up beside me.

"Susanna," he says, and I jump a foot off the ground.

He pulls off his sweatshirt and hands it to me. I bury my face in the fabric and muffle my sobs. He puts his arm around me and I turn into his chest, covered only by a thin T-shirt. Mashing the sweatshirt between us, I fight to control myself. "You should go home," Stu says kindly. "I have my cell and I'll call Mom to come get you."

Before he can fish his cell from his jeans pocket, I look up into his face. I see worry for me written in his eyes. Something blows in my heart. Without thinking about it, I throw my arms around his neck and kiss him square on his mouth. I cling to him, sealing my lips against his and tasting the salt of my own tears. When I break off, I toss down his sweatshirt and run as fast as I can back across the field.

Later at home, I relive what has happened. I kissed Stu, my friend since elementary school. I acted like a crazy person and cried like a baby, soaked his sweatshirt and all but told him how I feel about him. Now I'm so embarrassed I want to hide under a rock.

Mrs. Mendoza saw me running and caught me when I arrived at the parking lot. She put me in her car and drove me straight home. I'm glad to see that all the visitors are gone and our house is quiet. Mom thanks Mrs. Mendoza for bringing me home and closes the door. By now I've dried up, but it wouldn't take a rocket scientist to see that I've been crying hard.

"Want to talk?" Mom asks.

"Bree's dead," I say.

"That part's over now and we don't have to ever do it again." Mom looks resigned. "Would you like something to eat? There are casseroles and soups and Crock-Pots full of food on the kitchen counter. You'll feel better if you eat, Sissy."

Mom thinks everything can be fixed with

food. What she doesn't know is that my bad mood is about more than Bree. I've just made a fool of myself with Stu. "Later," I say.

She goes to bed and I sit in the dark and watch a candle glow on the coffee table. After a few minutes, I notice that my Christmas cactuses are drooping low in their pots. I turn on a lamp and see that they have bloomed and the flowers are so plentiful that they're dragging down the stems. The flowers are bright fuchsia. I touch the blossoms and feel weepy again.

This is the first time I've ever grown anything on my own that lived. And they decide to bloom on the day we bury my sister. I resent that they look so pretty when I feel so awful. I set them outside in the cold and go to bed.

# THIRTEEN

"She's a beauty," a nurse named Colleen says. She's standing next to me in the neonatal unit and we're looking down at Bree's baby inside the incubator. The baby's wearing a pink terry-cloth shirt, a hat and booties and a diaper. The pads and tape are gone from her eyes and the breathing mask has been removed. "Would you like to hold her?" Colleen asks.

I'm wearing a hospital-issue gown over my street clothes and I've scrubbed my hands with antibacterial soap. I nod and the nurse lifts the lid, unsnaps the lead wires on the baby's chest from a nearby machine and gently lifts her. Colleen coos, "Your aunt's here, baby girl."

My hands are shaky, but I take the baby. As I hold her stretched across my palms, I'm shocked at how small and weightless she feels.

"Hold her upright," Colleen says. "Talk to her."

What do I say to a baby? My mind goes blank. "Hello," I whisper.

The nurse reaches over and tickles the baby's chest. "When they're premature, you have to remind them to breathe." The baby squirms and I tighten my hold. "She's not as fragile as she looks. Go ahead and hold her closer."

I place her on my shoulder and she rests there, makes a little grunting sound that melts my heart. "What are the wires for? Is her heart okay?"

"Her heart's fine. The machine is a monitor for keeping tabs on her breathing. It beeps if she goes too long without taking a breath on her own. If the machine makes a noise, we jiggle her until she takes one."

"How long before she remembers to breathe without that monitor?" I'm wondering how we can take her home if she needs a monitor.

Colleen reads my mind. "Sometimes we send babies home with a monitor. We'll have to wait and see how she does." Colleen motions me to a platform atop a table. "Come over here and let me show you how to wrap her."

On the table warmed by lights, the nurse places the baby on a cotton blanket. I watch as she wraps her up like a moth in a cocoon and hands her back to me. "It's called swaddling. It keeps the baby snug and warm. Reminds them of the womb and comforts them. Now you try it."

I don't do a very good job and the blanket is sloppy and loose. While I try again, Mom shows up and watches over my shoulder. "I used to do this for you girls," she says.

"Did you bring her clothes?" I ask.

Mom is holding a small bag from the baby's nursery at home. Dr. Kendrow has told us the baby can wear her own clothes if we'd like to bring them to the hospital, and I've picked out two pairs of the cutest jammies. Bree bought them when she bought the furniture. I rewrap the baby blanket, this time more tightly, and pick up the baby. "She's about the size of a football," I say, laughing, and hold her out to Mom. "Your turn."

Mom glances at her bad hands. "Maybe I

should sit in that rocker and let you hand her to me."

Mom sits, holds the baby and begins to rock. I notice several rocking chairs in the unit.

Colleen explains. "We have volunteers who come in and hold the babies and rock them. Some of these preemies are here for months, and the birth mother may have kids at home and simply can't be here all the time. So these surrogate grandmothers take on the holding, rocking and feeding duties because babies need to be held and cuddled or they won't thrive."

I look around and see that some of the babies are way smaller than ours, and with many more machines around their incubators. I'm glad our baby is in better shape.

"Would you like to give her a bottle?" Colleen asks.

She gets one ready and instructs us to hold the baby upright when we feed her. The bottle looks like one I've used to feed my old dolls, but the nurse tells me these special bottles have small nipples because preemies have tiny mouths. Mom does the honors, but we have to keep waking our baby up. She'd rather sleep than eat.

As I watch, it hits me that I've stopped thinking about the baby as Bree's and begun thinking of her as ours. She *is* ours.

"It would be nice if she had a name," Mom says, aiming her words at me.

I shift from foot to foot. My job. "I'm still thinking," I say. "It needs to be right." I've discarded dozens of names already. None from the naming book seems to fit her.

Mom stares at the baby. "She looks like Bree."

Mom's hinting, but I don't think it's the thing to do. "It'll make us sad to call her Briana," I say.

"Probably so," Mom says with a sigh.

For once, Mom and I agree.

On Monday I have to face Stu at school. Melody too. I wonder if he's told her what I did. When I see them in the hall before the first bell, they have their heads together in private conversation. I panic. What if he's telling her right now? I rush up. "Hey there. What are you guys up to?" My voice sounds overly cheerful. "I got to hold the baby yesterday," I say before they can answer my first question.

"That's awesome," Melody says.

Stu hasn't said anything. He just looks at the floor.

To Melody, I say, "I'm going to ask your dad if I can ride into the city with him every day over the break. At Thanksgiving he said he'd give me a ride to the hospital and back."

"It's a plan," Melody says.

Is she being standoffish? I can't tell, so I say, "I'm asking the baby's doctor if you two can come up and see her."

"I'd *love* that," Melody says, suddenly all smiles. "We'll come together."

Stu won't make eye contact with me.

The bell rings and I'm glad because we've run out of things to say. "See you in band," Melody says, and heads off to homeroom.

I start off too, but Stu falls in step alongside me because, after all, we *are* in the same homeroom. My mouth goes dry. "I guess we should talk," he says.

"If it's about Saturday, forget it." I feel all squirmy, like bugs are crawling under my skin. "I was just having a meltdown. The funeral and all. Thanks for the loan of your sweatshirt. Hope I didn't ruin it."

"You're all right now?"

I flash him a smile. "Of course I'm all right. Good as new. How about you?"

He looks relieved. It hurts me that he looks so relieved. "I'm all right too. It was just that I didn't expect that to happen."

"Me either. Guess I lost it. Sorry." We're at the door of our classroom. I face him. "Friends?" I hold out my hand.

He takes my hand and shakes it. A grin lights up his face. "Always," he says.

I enter the room first, forcing myself to smile at kids as I walk to my seat. Inside, my heart is hurting. My kissing him hasn't meant a thing to him. Not one thing.

Our school concert goes off without a hitch— except for a first grader who barfs all over the stage during part one. Once it's cleaned up and the furor dies down, the program sails along without a hitch. I play my solo perfectly, thanks to so much practice, I'm sure, and afterward, Melody and her parents, Stu and his family and Mom and I go to the IHOP and gobble down pancakes.

When I ask Melody's dad for a ride to the hospital throughout the holiday school break, he says, "I'll pick you up Monday through Friday mornings at seven-fifteen and have you home by six."

That means no sleeping in from now until school starts again, but being with the baby is worth it to me. Mom asks, "Are you sure this is smart, Sissy? I mean, *every day?*"

She'll be busy tying up year-end accounting chores for many of her clients and won't come unless it's a weekend.

"Well, yes," I say, embarrassed that she brings it up now in front of everybody.

She doesn't mention it again until we're alone at home. "I think you should reconsider going to the hospital so much."

"Why? I want to be with her, and I have things to learn. . . . You know, how to take the most excellent care of her for when she comes home."

"But you're returning to school in January."

"Then it'll be your turn," I say, smiling. "And you've already got experience with babies. I don't."

"Sissy—"

"Oh, Mom, I don't mind losing a little sleep." I hug her from behind. "I'm going to be the best aunt in history. And don't worry. After school starts up again, I'll take charge every afternoon as soon as I get home."

I trot upstairs before Mom can say anything else and ruin my good mood.

On Tuesday Dr. Kendrow runs into me in the unit. "The nurses tell me you've taken up residency here." She smiles as she says it, so I know she's teasing me.

"I like being around our baby."

"Do you play your flute for her?"

I hadn't thought about it. "I'll bring it tomorrow." Before she can leave, I ask, "How's she doing?"

"She's doing well."

"I can't wait to take her home. Everything's ready and waiting for her."

"I'd like to see her gain a little more weight."

"She drinks all her bottle when I feed her," I say hopefully.

"And her blood work looks good too. Just a while longer. Be patient."

I ask, "Can two of my friends come and take

a peek at her? Just a quick peek. They won't be in the way."

Dr. Kendrow thinks about it, turns her smile on me. "Perhaps just a quick look. I'll let the nurses know you have permission. Just tell them before your friends descend on the place."

The hospital prefers that people not use cell phones on the floors, so I call Melody from an outside line at the nurses' station. I tell her about the okay to visit and she shrieks. "Really? I can't wait!"

"We can ride in with your dad and have breakfast in the hospital cafeteria," I suggest. "The waffles are great."

"Hang on," she says. "Let me see if Mom can come get us."

I wait, think about calling Stu and wonder if he'll want to come.

Moments later, Melody comes back on the line. "Mom says she'll pick us up because we still have some presents to buy, so we can go straight to the mall from the hospital. So it's a win-win situation. I get to see the baby. I get to shop." She pauses. "Do you want to come with us?"

It doesn't feel like a real invitation, like she

really wants me to come to the mall, but I want to stay at the hospital for the rest of the day anyway. "No," I tell her. "Colleen says I can give the baby a supervised sponge bath."

Melody says she'll call Stu and let him know. I'm disappointed, but Melody's taken it out of my hands. It's probably better anyway that I don't call him. I have to return to thinking of him as only a friend.

We hang up. A calendar at the nurses' station has the days crossed out in red, and I'm surprised to see that there are only five more days until Christmas. I haven't been keeping track at all.

I start to return to the unit, but instead stand rooted to the floor. Across the way, talking with Dr. Kendrow, I see a woman who looks familiar. In a nanosecond I recognize her. My mouth goes dry as I watch them cross to our baby's incubator and peer inside. It's the attorney who came to our house last fall. It's Sheila Watson.

# FOURTEEN

Before I hide, Ms. Watson looks up and sees me. She smiles, waves and heads straight to me. "Hello! You're Susanna, aren't you? Remember me—Sheila Watson?"

Reluctantly I nod.

"Briana's baby is just lovely. Her doctor tells me she's doing really well."

"How did you know about her? About her being born?" The inside of my mouth is dry as a desert and I can hardly get the words out.

"There was a write-up in the paper months ago. Your sister was something of a medical phenomenon, you know. Then I read in the obituary column that she had died, and I heard that her baby was in intensive care."

I hadn't read about Bree in the paper and no one had mentioned the article to me until now. My news comes from text messaging and e-mail, and it concerns my friends and school. Once in a while I watch the TV news, but it's usually pretty depressing, so I don't watch often.

One thing I've learned hanging around the hospital is that without a patient's approval no one on staff talks about a patient to the media, or for that matter, to anyone else who wants information. "How do you know Dr. Kendrow?" I'm bold now, asking questions I would have been too shy to ask months ago.

"I was told she's head of this unit."

"Why would she let you see our baby?"

"Because I was given permission to see her."

"Who gave you permission?"

Sheila smiles, reminding me of someone being indulgent with a very slow learner. "Why, your mother, of course."

I hit my front door with a bang, yelling, "Mom!"

She's in the kitchen warming a casserole for

our supper. "You don't have to shout, Sissy. There's nothing wrong with my hearing." She glances up, sees my face and, looking alarmed, asks, "What's wrong? Is it the baby?"

"Would you care?"

"What are you talking about? Yes, I care."

"Then why did you let that . . . that *lawyer* in to see her?"

Mom's face turns pink. "You saw Ms. Watson?"

"She was looking at Bree's baby. At *our* baby! She wants her, doesn't she? She's trying to get her from us! And you . . . and you . . ." I break down.

"She called, asked if she might go see the baby. I didn't see anything wrong with that."

"She has reasons for wanting to see her," I shout, "and you know what they are!"

Mom goes to the table, pulls out a chair and sits in another. "Sit down, Sissy. Let's talk."

I don't want to sit and talk. I want to scream. I go to the chair, though, and sit. "So talk."

"You have no idea how difficult it will be to raise a baby—"

"I told you I'll help raise her."

"You're fourteen—"

"Fifteen in March." I'm thinking she's going

to use immaturity as an argument against me, but she doesn't.

"And when you're eighteen you'll go to college, or off to begin a job. The baby will only be four years old. Think about that. And think about this too." She holds up her hands, the joints knotty with arthritis. "Look at me. I don't know if I can change her diapers, much less prepare her bottles, dress her, potty-train her, bake her birthday cakes." She shakes her head. "And Dr. Kendrow's told me that when she comes home, she'll need constant monitoring. She'll have to be fed every three hours. *Every three hours* around the clock, then every four hours, and so on until she can finally switch to 'on-demand' feeding. This can take months!"

I see that Mom's scared. I'm scared too. I'm scared of losing the baby, not of taking care of her. "We can't just give her away to strangers." My voice is quivering. "She's *family.*"

Mom goes so quiet, I hear the kitchen clock ticking off seconds across the room.

"I'll take the night shifts," I say stubbornly.

"You have no idea," she repeats. "The—the responsibility of it all."

I feel sorry for her, but I also have to fight for our baby. "We can do this, Mom. We have to *try*!"

Mom stares across the table—not at me, but at the wall behind me. "She's fragile, Sissy. What if——" She stops, starts again. "What if she—she dies? That can happen, you know, with a preemie. They can die of that sudden infant death syndrome. I—I can't lose another child, Sissy. I just can't."

Her face crumples like tissue paper and she starts to cry really hard. She buries her face in her hands and I watch her shoulders shake with every sob. I don't know what to do for her. There's nothing I *can* do for her. The hole Bree left in our lives and in Mom's heart is too big to fill. How can I expect a tiny baby to fill up such a deep, dark hole? I get up, leave Mom at the table and go to my room, where I cry too.

I act cheerful and happy the next day when Melody, Stu and I ride to the hospital together. I don't want anyone to know that Mom's considering giving our baby up for adoption. We ride the elevator up to the neonatal unit and Colleen meets us at the desk. "You must be Susanna's friends."

I introduce them and wash up. Melody and Stu wash their hands too. Babies are bundled in their plastic units, most of them red-faced and crying. They sound like mewing kittens. "Everybody's hungry," Colleen says. "And we're short-staffed today."

I lead Melody and Stu to our baby's incubator and see that she's sleeping through all the noise.

"Oh my gosh!" Melody says. "She's so little."

Stu just stands and stares.

My hands itch to hold her, but I don't, so we watch her sleep. Her stocking hat is pushed back, showing off her mass of black hair. Her tiny mouth makes sucking motions and I wonder if babies dream, and if they do, what could they dream about?

"When can you take her home?" Melody asks.

I'm glad I'm not looking her in the eye when I say, "Dr. Kendrow will decide, but remember, she wasn't supposed to be born until next month."

I hear a rumbling noise and we both look at Stu. "Sorry. I'm hungry," he says, red-faced.

Melody and I laugh, and I say, "Let's go eat."

On the way out of the unit, Melody stops

and stares at the smallest baby in there. He's surrounded by machines, and tubes are coming out of his mouth and nose. Melody's eyes go wide and unblinking. "Is—is he all right? I've never seen anything so tiny."

I know a little bit about him because I hang around all day. "He was born way too early," I tell her. "His mom was only twenty-eight weeks along when she had him."

"How old is he now?"

"Three weeks old. He's got a lot of catching up to do."

"Can he catch up?" This from Stu, whose hand is almost twice the size of the baby's whole body.

I remember that Bree's baby was around twenty-eight weeks when her aneurysm burst. Still, Bree held on to her baby for another seven weeks. "I don't know," I say to Stu. "I just know he's got a long way to go. He'll be here for months."

"Why's that tube in his mouth?" Melody asks.

"It's a feeding tube because he's too little to suck a bottle. The one coming from his nose is giving him oxygen." Both Stu and Melody stare down at the baby and I can tell that they're upset. I've come here for days, been at Bree's bedside for weeks before this. I've seen things other girls my age rarely see, and I have a perspective that far exceeds that of my friends. I feel like we've been running a race and I've sprinted ahead of them, taken a shortcut that was rocky and hard and that's left me bruised. Now I've arrived at the finish line ahead of them and have to wait for them to catch up. "Come on." I hook my arms through theirs. "The waffles here are pretty good."

The cafeteria smells warm and buttery. It's full of people—residents in green scrubs, visitors, hospital workers. The clatter of trays and cups mingle with the low buzz of voices. We get in line and I force myself to buy food I know I can't eat just to keep my happy act going. We pay the cashier and find a table in the middle of the hubbub. "When's your mom coming?" I ask as we settle down.

"Nine-fifteen," Melody says.

It's eight-thirty now. Stu seems awfully quiet, and I'm wondering if he's self-conscious around me. I hope not. My feelings for him have taken a backseat to the baby and the prospect of giving her up. I'm pushing a piece of waffle into my mouth when I notice that Melody and Stu have stopped talking and are watching me. "What?" I say. "Did I dribble syrup?"

They're sitting across from me, their shoulders touching. I look from one to the other.

Melody clears her throat. "I . . . um . . . we have something to tell you."

I see their expressions. Both look nervous. My heart begins to thud with a kind of dread. Whatever's going on is going to slam me, and I know it. I set down my fork, wait for the hammer that's about to fall. "Tell me."

Melody glances at Stu, reaches over and laces her fingers through his. "We—Stu and I are . . . going out."

Her admission hangs in the air between us. *Going out.* A way to announce they are dating exclusively. That they're boyfriend-girlfriend. A couple. Together. More than just friends. I bounce my gaze from face to face. This isn't a joke. "How long?" I ask, and hope I sound curious, not devastated.

"A while," Melody says, biting her lower lip. "Since the summer."

Pictures flash in my mind like a deck of cards being shuffled. I see Melody and Stu at the pool, their towels inches apart . . . rubbing suntan lotion on each other . . . the looks they gave each other at the tree sale . . . their constant togetherness. I remember Halloween, and the way they were both "busy," and I'm certain now that they had been busy with each other. *How could I have been so stupid as not to catch on before now?* I can't look at Stu, so I concentrate on Melody. "Why did you wait until now to tell me?"

"There was never a good time. With all that was happening to you . . . well, we just didn't know how."

"Or when," Stu adds. His face has gone blank.

They're asking me to make their confession acceptable. To give them my blessing. Our threesome is breaking up—them the Dynamic Duo, me the Lone Ranger.

"Please say something." Melody looks pale and scared. "You're my best friend, Susanna."

I understand scared. I know scared. "It isn't a crime to fall in love," I finally say.

"Really?" Hope crosses Melody's face.

I think, *Bree said she was in love with Jerry*.

"Then it's okay?" Melody asks. "You're not mad at us?"

"Not mad." I'm sad. Horribly sad, but I can't tell her that. Something is passing away, like autumn leaves blown from trees by the winds of change. I stand. "I need to get back upstairs. I need to feed Bree's baby. She's probably awake now. And hungry."

"Can we talk later?"

"Call me."

"But we're still friends?" Melody looks skeptical.

Did she think I'd explode and dump on her? I know what she wants me to say, and I know what I must tell her. In a steady voice, I say, "We'll always be friends."

I go to the lobby, but don't take the elevator. Instead I take the stairs, run up the stairwell until my legs throb and my lungs feel fiery and ready to burst. But I run up all eleven flights without stopping.

# FIFTEEN

In the stairwell, I sag against the wall and wait
to catch my breath. My calf muscles are
screaming from the exertion, but all I can think
about are my two best friends changing the
rules and becoming boyfriend-girlfriend. I want
to feel angry. I want to hate them for liking each
other behind my back. Yet if I'd had my way, if
Stu had fallen for me, wouldn't it be Melody
who would be left out in the cold? I think about
her heart hurting the way mine is and realize I
don't want her to feel this way. I don't want
anyone to feel this way.

Which brings me full circle to thoughts of

my sister. Bree had such dreams and plans for herself and Jerry. If they had stayed together, if she had stayed in L.A., the aneurysm would still have happened—that's what Dr. Franklin has told us. And Jerry might not have agreed to keep her alive on machines. And the baby would have never been born. I shudder thinking about it. And I know deep down that I'd rather know that Bree's baby—our baby—is alive, even if she's adopted and has to live with other people.

I start to cry over the sense of loss that's fallen on me like dark rain. From below, I hear a stairwell door open, then hear footsteps ascending. I quickly wipe my cheeks and push through the door of the eleventh floor. The warm air hits my face and I realize how cold I've gotten in the unheated stairwell. The warmth makes me feel better.

Colleen waves as I pass the desk and go into the unit. Bree's baby is in her incubator and she's crying—screaming, actually. I see a round Band-Aid taped to her tiny heel. "The lab tech just drew blood," Colleen says, coming alongside me. "Why don't you swaddle her and hold her?"

I open the lid and pick her up, but she continues to cry. I wrap her tightly in the blanket, put her back into her incubator because I know I should start letting go of her if Mom's going to allow her to be adopted. I spy my flute case on the floor, drag a rocking chair over to the side of the baby's bubble and open my case.

I lift my flute, hold the silver instrument up and play "What Child Is This?" because that's the first song that pops into my head. I get into the music and play the song a second time, and soon the room fades and I'm lost in my music.

At some point, when I rest for a minute, Colleen says, "You play beautifully."

I thank her.

She says, "Look," and gestures at the plastic shell.

I turn and see that the baby has stopped crying and she's looking straight at me. And even though I know newborns can't see really well, I swear she's staring, her slate-colored eyes full of curiosity, her head cocked as if she's listening, and knows who I am. That I am Susanna, her aunt, maker of music. My heart swells. I raise the flute to my lips and play again.

• • •

When I get home that night, the house is dark
except for a glow in front of the living room
window. Once inside, I see that the glow is
coming from a fully decorated Christmas tree.
Not our pathetic old artificial tree, but a fresh
live one. The pine scent fills the room. On the
table, I find a note from Mom.

> *Sissy,*
>       *The tree is courtesy of your friends, Melody
> and Stuart and Mr. and Mrs. Mendoza. They
> showed up with it this afternoon and asked per-
> mission to set it up and completely decorate it.
> How could I say no? Plus you deserve a tree. We
> should have a tree!*
>       *I'm with a client until seven, then I'll be
> home. Warm yourself something from the fridge.
> And Stuart asked me to have you please call him
> as soon as you get home.*
>
>                                     *Love,*
>                                     *Mom*

I go to my room and call Stu. He answers on the
second ring. Has he been waiting by the phone?
"Hey. It's me," I say.

"Thanks for calling."

"Thanks for the tree. I mean that. It's really nice."

"It was Mellie's idea and the Mendozas wanted to help."

*A guilt offering?* I wonder.

"We thought you should have a tree." He wants to say something else, so I wait on the line letting the silence stretch until he breaks it. "I'm sorry it took us . . . Mellie and me . . . so long to tell you about our dating."

*Us.* The new way of seeing my two best friends. Us, not we. "I'm over it," I say. Not quite the truth, but I know I *will* get over it, so I say so because I think he needs to hear it.

"I . . . um . . . I want you to know something, Susanna."

I've always liked to hear him say my name.

"I never said anything to Melody about what happened between us after the funeral. And I never will."

I'm glad, but curious. "Why?"

"I just don't think she needs to know, that's all."

He was protecting her.

"She . . . she would never understand and I

don't want her to be mad at you. And I don't want you to think for a minute that it didn't mean something to me. It did."

He was protecting me.

"I'll forget it if you will," I say.

Another silence. "I guess I'll see you later."

"Later," I say, and hang up. I sit still and search my feelings, and say goodbye to my first serious crush. I'm okay about it.

I fall asleep on my bed fully clothed before Mom gets home and wake at six the next morning. I quickly take a shower and get ready for Melody's dad to pick me up. When I go downstairs, Mom is sitting on the sofa, a large white box on her lap. "Sorry I conked out that way," I tell her. "You could have woken me up."

"I looked in on you and didn't have the heart."

"I like the tree."

"It was very thoughtful of your friends. I like it too."

I glance at the box. "Do you want me to wrap that for you this afternoon?"

"It isn't a gift."

I sit beside her and peek into the open box. It's filled with ribbons, barrettes, scrunchies, headbands and bows. "What's this?"

"Your and Bree's hair gear from when you were little."

I forage through the pile. "You saved all these?"

"It's what mothers do." She picks up a sparkling headband with streamers and stars glued on. "This was your sister's favorite. She was a fairy princess every time she put it on. Which was every day when she was three. She had a wand too, but it broke in half. How she cried."

The box holds other treasures. I find a baby bracelet made of beads with letters that spell my name. I can't believe my wrist was ever this small. I pick up a pie plate of hardened plaster of paris, the impression of a child's handprint painted gold pressed in its center.

"Bree's," Mom says. "From her nursery school on Mother's Day."

On the back is a poem. Aloud I read, "'This is to remind you, / When I have grown so tall, / That once I was quite little, / And my hands were very small.'"

Mom's eyes fill with tears. "I talked to Ms. Watson yesterday," she says.

I sit stock-still and hear the sound of my heart thumping with dread. Can Mom hear it too?

"I told her that while it makes a lot of sense to have a good, loving couple raise Bree's baby, I—*we* can't let her go. She's all we have of Bree. All that remains of my lovely daughter."

I get light-headed with relief. I want to jump up and down and shout out how happy I am. I don't, though. I slip my arms around Mom. She kisses my forehead, lays her cheek against my hair. "I talked to Dr. Kendrow too, and she says we can bring the baby home day after tomorrow. On Christmas Eve."

"We can?" I can't contain myself and bounce up and down on the couch.

Mom shakes her head and with a smile says, "You're *really* going to have to come up with a name for her, Sissy."

# SIXTEEN

During the ride home from the hospital, I sit in the backseat next to the strapped-in carrier holding the baby. We have dressed her in pink and lavender and she's all scrunched up, sound asleep. Mom keeps glancing in the rearview mirror and asking, "Is she all right?"

"She's fine."

In the trunk, we have a home monitor to track her breathing and a going-home bag from the hospital full of formula, diapers, baby wipes and other baby products—all we need to get started. Melody's already informed me that her mother is having a huge baby shower for us just as soon as she can get it organized. We are all surprised that Dr. Kendrow has allowed the baby to leave the hospital so soon, but she's gained enough weight and although she still needs to be monitored, her lungs are developed enough for her to go.

"We've got plans," Melody has told me on the phone. "Do you know how many people are volunteering to help your mom when you go back to school? It's true. Mom's got a long list. So . . . can I come over on Christmas Day? Can I hold her? I'm her surrogate aunt, you know."

I tell her yes because I feel generous and big-hearted. We're still best friends and the baby will grow up with her and Stu hanging around.

Traffic is heavy and by the time we get home, it's dark. I change and feed the baby and walk around the house, showing her the place, talking to her while holding her on my shoulder. She's alert and seems to be looking at everything. She's especially attracted to the lights on the tree.

Later I put her in her crib and drag my sleeping bag into her room.

Mom asks, "What are you doing?"

"I think I'll sleep on the floor next to her bed tonight."

"Are you sure? It's going to be cold."

I've thrown several blankets on the floor and have slipped on my flannel pj's, the ones with Dalmatians all over them. "Just for tonight."

The monitor is set up and I have an alarm clock to wake me so that I can give her a bottle in three hours.

"I don't mind taking a feeding shift," Mom says.

"I'll handle it tonight," I tell her.

We settle down, the baby in her crib and me on the floor. From the floor, my perspective is different. Through the window, I see stars dotting the night sky. They look cold and far away. A cow-jumping-over-the-moon night-light glows from a nearby wall socket. I see a baseboard left unpainted from when I abruptly stopped the night Bree was taken to the hospital.

The baby sleeps, but I can't. I turn on my clock radio, tune it to a station that plays holiday music all night long on Christmas Eve without any interruptions. I think the baby likes music. Maybe I'll teach her how to play the flute someday.

As I listen and wait for sleep, one particular carol performed by a symphony orchestra catches my ear. I sit upright, my eyes wide open, suddenly knowing what I'm going to name the baby. Why didn't I think of it before?

*Noel.* It means Christmas and she's the most wonderful Christmas gift of all. I decide that she needs her mother's name too, so that she'll always remember who she came from. She'll be Briana Noel, but we'll call her Noel. I say the name aloud and it settles on my heart like firelight, and I know it's right. So right for her. I can't wait to tell Mom.

Through the window the stars twinkle, no longer cold-looking, but only bright and beautiful and full of promise.

*Noel!*

# About the Author

LURLENE McDANIEL began writing inspirational novels about teenagers facing life-altering situations when her son was diagnosed with juvenile diabetes. "I want kids to know that while people don't get to choose what life gives to them, they do get to choose how they respond."

Lurlene McDaniel's novels are hard-hitting and realistic, but also leave readers with inspiration and hope. Her books have received acclaim from readers, teachers, parents, and reviewers. Her novels *Don't Die, My Love; I'll Be Seeing You;* and *Till Death Do Us Part* have all been national bestsellers.

Lurlene McDaniel lives in Chattanooga, Tennessee.

*You'll want to read*

# Letting Go of Lisa

*Lisa has a tragic secret, and when she decides
she'll handle it herself, Nathan has to
make a choice. Can he ever let go of Lisa?*